THE ROMULANS IN PURSUIT

"The Romulans continue to pursue, Captain," Spock reported. "And they are increasing their speed."

"Can we outrun them, Mr. Spock?"

Spock hesitated, studying readouts as fast as the battle computer could supply them. "Indeterminate, Captain. With three ships in pursuit, prediction becomes extremely complex."

"Captain," Uhura interrupted. "I've received an incoming transmission from the commander of the Romulan force. He seems anxious to talk to you."

"I'll bet," Kirk replied. "Put him through . . . I've got a couple of things to talk over with him!"

STAR TREK
LOG SIX

Alan Dean Foster

Based on the Popular Animated Series Created
by Gene Roddenberry

BALLANTINE BOOKS ● NEW YORK

Library of Congress Catalog Card Number: 74-8477

ISBN 0-345-24855-1-150

Manufactured in the United States of America

First Ballantine Books Edition: March, 1976

Cover art supplied by Filmation Associates

For Lou Mindling . . .

Expediter, friend, oasis in the desert of
deviltry and dementia, and all-around human being.

CONTENTS

STAR TREK LOG SIX

Log of the Starship *Enterprise*

Stardates 5532.8 — 5535.2 Inclusive

James T. Kirk, Capt., USSC, FS, ret.

Commanding

transcribed by
Alan Dean Foster

At the Galactic Historical Archives
on S. Monicus I
and
Frontier Outpost Moran
stardated 6111.3

For the Curator: JLR

PART I

ALBATROSS

(Adapted from a script by Dario Finelli)

I

It had form but faint substance, shape but little color, face but no visage.

Body but no soul.

Its sword was an extension of its own right arm and it moved and danced with a grace and fluidity that was not human.

Sulu parried and thrust, beat and lunged with his own insulated blade. Initially he had been casual in attack, though his tenebrous opponent made up in nimbleness what it lacked in knowledge and experience.

But it was rapidly absorbing every trick Sulu the fencing master could think of—memorizing each one, analyzing its weaknesses and strong points, and then using them on Sulu in return. It had not yet mastered the subtle intricacies of multiple combinations, thus preventing the *Enterprise*'s helmsman from being skewered a dozen times over.

But since Sulu's opponent did not tire, the combat loomed as increasingly unequal.

Sulu relished the contest. Never before had he faced so dangerous a fighter, nor one so eerily beautiful. His luminescent antagonist shone like a billion golden glowmites in the light of the room. Though its skull was featureless, it did not lack eyes.

Those enigmatic orbs kept close watch on the helmsman's movements, on the placement of his feet, on the way he held his balancing back hand, and most especially on the tip of that deadly foil.

Sulu feinted low, then went high with the point of

his blade. As his opponent moved his blade up to parry, the helmsman shot his left leg out in a strong side kick.

The gilded wraith knocked the point aside and lunged forward to finish the fight. But instead of skipping back out of range, Sulu stood his ground, shot vertically into the air and executed a perfect jump-spinning back kick. His shoe struck the sword-arm, smashing it aside, while his foil whipped around simultaneously to stab straight through that gleaming, glittering throat ...

The attacker froze as Sulu withdrew his blade. No blood had gushed forth on contact, no stream of molten yellow fluid. There had been only an indifferent buzz at the mortal blow.

Walking away from his paralyzed opponent, Sulu picked a towel off a nearby bench and mopped at his sweating face.

"The computer annex's getting too clever, Mr. Scott. It's getting harder and harder to think up new combinations to use against it."

Chief Engineer Montgomery Scott nodded as he pressed the switch on the makeshift control panel. Sulu's dervishlike opponent, a man-shape given form and body by ionized gas held in a rigorously restricted force-field, disappeared—a solid-state djinn.

"I don't see why you've never used that kick-parry before," Scott observed. "It worked marvelously."

Sulu smiled as he toweled the back of his neck. "Never had to get that fancy before. Trouble is, the computer rarely lets me get away with a successful move more than once." He let out a short sigh.

"The problem with that defense is that if you miss the parry-kick, you're left floating in mid-air with your sword at your side—a ripe candidate for shish kebab." His expression turned studious.

"Its movements are still a little unnatural, still a bit machinelike. And I noticed a few other problems, too. There were several times when it fought while floating a couple of centimeters above the floor." He grinned. "No fair. The computer's got enough advantages as it is."

"Not enough to reduce the experience of actual combat, though," Scott countered, checking a tiny window in the panel. "You're still well ahead, laddie, twelve touches to five."

"I remember when I used to beat it seventeen to nothing. It's learning, all right."

Scott shrugged. "That's one of the functions of a games computer. If I could program the ship's computer, you'd have a mechanical fighter who'd act perfectly human, even to experiencing fatigue as the battle wore on. But you know what the captain would say if we asked for ship computation time for a project like this." He indicated the wire-fringed control panel.

"I had a bit of a snap with the stores records cagin' the material for this—filed the requisitions under the 'emergency repairs' column. Shouldn't be any trouble with it unless Starfleet springs a surprise inventory on us. But usin' the main computer—," he shook his head firmly, "we've as much chance of that as me grandmother has of throwin' the caber in the next interstellar Highland games."

Sulu accepted the engineer's declaration as he straightened his blade. The foil was insulated on pommel and blade, leaving only the metal tip uncovered. Whenever that naked point intersected the ionized gas in the force field, it registered as a touch on the control box Scott had rigged. Unfortunately, there was no equally accurate way of judging when his computer-controlled opponent scored a hit on him. For now, that had to be done visually. But the system was new, and Scott was still working on that problem as well as on several others.

They would have plenty of time during this long, dull mission to Draymia to perfect his *katana-to-ashi* opponent. Unlike say, Mr. Spock, who could always find plenty of challengers for tri-dimensional chess and other logic games, there wasn't anyone else on board who possessed more than a perfunctory knowledge of the modern martial art, which merged European-style fencing with the old karate of the Orient. Those crew members who were athletically inclined preferred bowling, or a good round of water polo.

When he'd finally grown deathly bored with fencing and kicking at his own shadow, Sulu had gone to Scott to see if the circuit-wizard could concoct something in the way of a robotic fighter. It hadn't taken the chief engineer long to produce his golden-gas hominoid.

Scott cocked an eyebrow as he glanced up from re-integrating one of the tiny modular components which controlled the fluidity of the force-field. Sulu was at the open arms cabinet.

"More, Lieutenant? Aren't you worn out yet?"

"Just a little saber work."

The engineer looked disapproving. "The final flurry? You know this thing can't score saber near as well as foil. Half the time I've no idea whether you're hittin' the target or not, with all that blade area. Let alone when it's hittin' you."

"Just a few minutes," Sulu pleaded. "I don't want my edge work to get rusty."

"All right, then, if you must." Scott didn't quite grumble. "I've the little matter of a ship to watch over."

He pressed a switch on the panel. Instantly, still frozen in the pose of its last execution, Sulu's antagonist glowed to life again. Scott adjusted controls, manipulated dials. The games computer set the newly programmed tape in motion and the lambent duelist assumed an *en garde* position.

Sulu lined up across from it. "Ready," he announced, turning his gaze to the gilded ghost. Scott touched a red switch.

The chief engineer had been right, though. At times Sulu himself couldn't tell whether or not he was slipping the first blow in. In a real fight, however, it would be more than merely satisfying to know whether a certain move worked. It would be vital.

The fight lasted only the few minutes Sulu had asked for, but not for the reasons originally given. His nebulous opponent had just performed a good parry, faked high and thrust low. Sulu had fallen for the feint. He jumped, trying to avoid a supposedly high attack. When he saw it was really going low, he attempted to recover by twisting in mid-air to kick-block downward, and got himself confused.

Trying simultaneously to parry with his own sword, the net result turned out to be a neat slash with the metal blade across the thin shoe he was wearing. He came down on both feet, immediately dropped the saber and buckled to the floor, wincing.

Having registered an undeniable score, the computer-controlled figure paused and resumed the ready position, awaiting the command to reengage once more.

Scott flicked it out of existence. There was a brief, dying whine as the force-field's power was cut. Then the engineer hurried over to where the helmsman sat, trying to unsnap the latches on his right shoe.

"Maybe you ought to go back to shadow-fightin', Sulu."

The helmsman grimaced as he worked at the latchings.

"Very funny, Mr. Scott."

Both men saw that the top of the shoe was already stained red. The humor of the situation was relegated to the background.

Scott put one hand on the heel, took a gentle grip on the toe with the other. "Easy, lad ... I'll try and get this off."

While he pushed and pulled, Sulu leaned back on both hands, stared at the ceiling of the gymnasium chamber and tried to think of other things. He couldn't repress a little gasp as the shoe finally slipped free.

There was a three-centimeter long gash across the top of his foot. Though it bled profusely, Sulu still counted himself lucky. The blade had struck at an angle which caused it to miss the big tendons. He made no move to rise.

"Stay there," Scott ordered him. He moved to a nearby cabinet and came back with a first-aid kit. The bandaging was crude, but at least they halted the flow of blood.

"Sorry, Sulu," he apologized when the temporary repair job was finished. "I'm much better with a needle-point welding laser."

Sulu eyed him archly. "Thanks just the same, Scotty, I'll settle for the bandages."

"Can you walk, or d'you want me to call for a stretcher?"

"No—no stretcher!" Sulu objected quickly. "The captain's liable to hear about it." He struggled to his feet. "Cut's on the top, not the sole. I can make it. Give me a hand to Sick Bay."

Scott mumbled about the waste of time as he helped Sulu get a large sock over the injured foot. Sulu was right, though. The captain wouldn't take kindly to the news that one of his Bridge officers had disabled himself at a game.

The few personnel they encountered in the corridors inquired solicitously as to the cause of the helmsman's limp. It was explained that he had slightly sprained an ankle playing handball. Much to Sulu's relief, this explanation seemed to be accepted by all.

McCoy was in a testier mood than usual. He unwrapped Scott's makeshift bandage job and stared disgustedly at the neat wound, muttering to himself as he went about the business of cleaning it out and closing it up.

"You cut your foot *how?*"

Sulu looked away and repeated the story for the third time.

"I've already told you, Dr. McCoy. Mr. Scott was kind enough to use some of his off-duty hours to develop an artificial warrior for me to practice against. I was making a parry where I shouldn't have been and I cut myself, that's all."

McCoy shook his head as he used three tiny organic clips to clamp the edges of the wound together. Spray from a can coated the wound and clips with an anesthetizing sealant. Eventually, the modified protein clips would be absorbed by Sulu's body, but not until the wound had completely healed over.

"That's a fairly deep cut, Helmsman," McCoy commented as he put away the can. "Try not to kick anyone with that foot till it heals up, hmmm? It should be okay."

Sulu looked as if he had something further to say,

but instead glanced at Scott for help. The chief engineer looked indifferent, then abruptly remembered how many times his senior officer had bailed him out of a difficult situation.

"Uh, Dr. McCoy . . . ."

McCoy looked back at him.

"We'd kinna hoped you wouldn't mention this little episode to the captain. I know it has to be entered in the medical log, but the lieutenant would appreciate it if you didn't go out of your way to tell him about it. You know what his reaction'd be."

"More than 'It'll be okay'," the doctor muttered. He didn't look at Sulu as he added, "I haven't got time anyway—not with that ton of medical supplies we're to deliver to Draymia to check out."

Glad for the change of subject and, incidentally, curious, Sulu swung his legs off the table and wondered, "Why should you have to bother with them at all, Doctor? Aren't they prepacked and self-contained?"

In reply McCoy sat down before a viewscreen and manipulated the controls. Peering over his shoulder, both Scott and Sulu saw vast columns of words and figures, massed tightly together like the ranks of an advancing army. McCoy gestured in an uncomplimentary manner at the screen, shaking his head dolefully.

"The instructional manuals for the equipment and supplies are all mixed up. If I don't get them properly relabeled before we arrive, the Draymians won't be able to tell an encephalograph from an endocrine monitor, or a case of Draymian aspirin from the serum for treating brain damage." He angrily snapped the picture off, turned to them.

"Whoever precoordinated this shipment's a likely candidate for a good shot of the latter drug."

"Can't you get someone to take over your regular assignments until you get everything sorted out?" Scott asked.

McCoy stared back at him evenly. "Would you want me to delegate my duties to someone else? Suppose Sulu had really sliced himself up? Or you, Scotty? How would you feel if I was off cataloging packages someplace?"

Neither man said anything.

He switched the screen back on, swiveled around to stare at the new display. "Besides, the health of hundreds of thousands of intelligent beings might depend on the safe delivery of these supplies. I'm not about to entrust their proper delivery to anyone but myself.

"Now if you don't mind," he growled, "I'd like to get back to my *important* work."

Sulu grinned as he gingerly put more weight on his injured limb. It was amazing how much better it felt already, after McCoy's precise ministrations.

The doctor's surface gruffness deceived neither of them.

"He'll make it all right, if he has to push himself double-shift," Scott declared as the two men entered the corridor outside Sick Bay. "He's got a good two weeks' ship-time before we make orbit around Draymia. It's only stardate fifty-five . . ."

". . . thirty-two point eight," Kirk finished, his voice slightly hoarse from the dry atmosphere of Draymia. As he spoke into the communicator, it relayed his voice back to the official log recorder on board the *Enterprise,* now orbiting far overhead.

"Preparing to beam back aboard ship following successful delivery of medical equipment and supplies to the planet Draymia in the Draymian star system. Kirk out . . ."

They stood on a balcony outside the chambers of the Draymian capital city administration, awaiting the arrival of the Supreme Prefect for the final embarkation ceremony. While Spock and McCoy discussed some obscure point of Draymian physiology as it related to certain of the supplies they had brought, Kirk turned and allowed his gaze to roam over the capital's skyline. Once one became used to the size of everything, built to nearly one and a quarter human scale, this world looked almost familiar. This, despite its extreme distance from the nearest Federation outpost planet.

The vegetation here was not terribly alien, likewise the animal life. But the hue of sky was just a touch too green, the tree trunks a bit too orange, the flying creatures' wings too scaly for hominess. In other words, Draymia was one of those many humanoid worlds whose weirdness was all the more disturbing for its elusive familiarity.

It wasn't a world where the local ungulates rolled around on wheels instead of walking on normal legs, or where the vegetation grew upside down like the ostrich forest on Olibaba. No, on a world like Draymia you always had the feeling that if you could just hit the right switch inside your head, there would be a little click, the proper lens would slip into place in front of your eyes, and everything would suddenly slide over into the normal.

"Hail, Captain Kirk! Hail, Mr. Spock!"

The men turned to see two Draymians emerging from the arched doorway. Kirk recognized the Supreme Prefect, but not his companion.

"Who's the other with him, Mr. Spock?"

"We met him briefly once before, Captain, on arrival," the first officer whispered, wondering idly why there had been no hearty hail for Dr. McCoy. Probably the Draymians simply hadn't noticed him yet. He filed the observation away for future consideration. "The being's name is Demos. He is the chief of the planetary security forces. He was in charge of receiving the few military-related medical supplies."

"Oh, yes," Kirk muttered. "I remember now." He broke off as both aliens halted before them. Their expressions—insofar as Kirk could now judge them—were neutral. Part of the ceremony of departure, no doubt.

Two and a half meters tall, well proportioned, the enormous humanoids could have appeared threatening. Their bulbous pop-eyes, however, gave their faces a comic cast which detracted from their massiveness.

As Kirk watched, the Supreme Prefect flicked one ear forward. The other was turned backward, perhaps to listen to some distant conversation. The effect, alongside the smooth pate, was startling. The Draymians possessed independently mounted ears, like the eyes of an Earthly chameleon.

The Prefect launched straight into the departure ceremony, as the somber-seeming Demos stood at attention at his side. The ceremony itself contained no surprises. Much was said about expanding trade and cooperation between Draymia and the Federation. There were words of mutual praise for the technical accomplishments of both civilizations, assurances of continuing friendship and interdependence, veiled polite references to those misguided races (who shall remain nameless) who might seek to interpose themselves between the goal of Federation-Draymian brotherhood, and so on.

Kirk and Spock replied where necessary, exchanging diplomatic banter with the aplomb and experience of men accustomed to far more complex goings-on. Kirk recalled one world on which merely saying a simple goodbye involved two days of feasting and athletic competition.

Finally, both the Prefect and Demos performed little half-bows and extended their hands, palms turned upward and open. "We wish to thank," he told them in his gravelly voice, "you and the rest of your Federation for your most welcome and invaluable assistance, Captain Kirk, in this and all matters."

The three men returned the gesture, which signified the taking of final farewell, as Kirk replied, "We hope through our medical assistance programs to develop and strengthen relations with all advanced civilizations such as your own, Supreme Prefect."

With that said, both humans and Draymians returned to a natural stance.

Kirk smiled easily, glanced back at his companions as he pulled out his communicator and flipped it open. "Shall we, Spock, Bones? Kirk to *Enterprise*—beam us aboard, Scotty."

The Prefect extended a hand, palm down this time, fingers bent at the middle knuckles. "If you would be so kind, Captain, a moment . . ."

Kirk hesitated uncertainly, then looked at Spock and McCoy. Both stared back at him blankly. The gestures were unmistakable, Spock seemed to say. Once the gesture of final leave-taking is made, nothing is supposed to follow.

Something of importance was happening here.

"Belay that, Mr. Scott," he said hurriedly into the open comm. He flipped it shut—for the moment.

"We await," he told the Supreme Prefect.

That appeared to satisfy the huge humanoid. He relaxed visibly and made a gesture to his companion that none of the humans recognized.

"Proceed, Commander Demos."

The security chief, with some ceremony, removed a folded sheet of opaque yellow plastic from a tunic pocket beneath his arm. It opened into the triangle favored by the Draymians.

"I have here a warrant," he announced solemnly, "in your own language, received by deep-space relay for the arrest and trial of one of your crew, Captain." He extended the yellow sheet toward Kirk, who stared at the smooth geometric form in disbelief.

"Best take it, Captain," Spock finally prompted him.

"Warrant," Kirk murmured dazedly. "Who . . . ?"

"If you would be so kind as to read it aloud, please, Captain?" the Prefect requested politely.

Kirk's gaze turned down to the plastic. On it was what looked to be a perfect xerographic copy of the familiar rectangle of official starfleet command-level stationary. The format design and intricate curlicued seals bordering it were either genuine or else the finest counterfeit he'd ever seen.

"You are directed to surrender," he read in a monotone, "for trial by the people of Draymia. Dr. Leonard McCoy, medical officer, *U.S.S. Enterprise* assigned your command . . ." His voice trailed away.

"Let me see that please, Captain," Spock requested rapidly. Rather more rapidly than was normal for him.

Blank-faced, Kirk handed the document over. His gaze slowly swung around to McCoy.

"Well, Bones . . . ?"

McCoy gaped back at him in open-mouthed confusion and could only shake his head slowly in total bewilderment. He had seen the opaque triangle of plastic, seen the inscribed borders and seals and the signatures at the bottom. But all he could do was stammer to the chief of Draymian security, "This has to be some kind of . . . bad joke."

"While there are those among you who might find certain aspects of our sense of humor peculiar," the giant replied stonily, "believe me when I say. that we do not consider the wanton slaughter of thousands of innocent civilians a joke."

McCoy's jaws made more movements than were necessary to produce the stumbling response. "Slaughter . . . thousands of people . . . ?"

Spock tapped the plastic sheet. "According to this, it is claimed that Dr. McCoy was responsible for a plague which ravaged the Draymian colony on Dramia II some nineteen years ago, Captain."

Kirk shook his head violently, then snatched the warrant from Spock's hands. "Let me see that thing again!" Once more his eyes roved over it, paying particular attention to the concluding seals and signatures. He glanced up at Demos, his voice barely controlled, and cold.

"This is a copy. I'd like to see the genuine article."

Demos executed the Draymian equivalent of a shrug, stepped aside. "Naturally, Captain. I would not expect you do to otherwise. The orginal is inside, properly protected. This is why we arranged for you to take your leave of us here." He gestured at the building.

"Welcome to the Draymian Chamber of Contemplative Reconstruction, Captain."

"Treachery, you mean," Kirk rumbled, as he stalked off toward the open portal.

Demos' eyes bulged even more than was natural as he followed alongside. "Justice, *we* mean," he glowered. "Under the circumstances, Captain Kirk, I think we are showing remarkable restraint."

"Restraint? I'll show you some restraining!" Kirk muttered tightly. "The *Enterprise* can 'restrain' this whole city."

"Doubtless your words hold truth," the Prefect observed from behind him as they entered the building once again. "We are a practical people. I, personally, am well aware of the destructive capabilities of your vessel. We are also an astute people psychologically.

"While you could probably reduce this city to its foundations, Captain Kirk, I've no doubt you will not. You will do nothing. Your reputation has preceded you. We know of your respect for your own laws. And as you have seen, the warrant is perfectly in order and properly approved by your own superiors. You will not disobey their orders."

"Not *my* superiors," Kirk shot back. "Not in Starfleet. This is a judicial order, issued by administrative authority."

"Whatever the source, Captain," Demos put in, "you recognize its authority. You will not attempt to contravene it. Therefore, I am certain you will offer no resistance while I perform my necessary duty." He reached out and placed a huge hand on McCoy's right shoulder.

"Dr. Leonard McCoy, I place you under official restraint. Do you yield voluntarily?"

McCoy nodded slowly and moved forward when Demos tugged, but the motions were independent of any real thought. He could only turn to gape wordlessly at Spock and Kirk as they followed.

There was a buzz for attention from Kirk's belt as they moved through the glass and stone structure, past languidly strolling Draymians bent on other official missions.

Kirk opened the communicator, his voice thick. "Kirk here."

"Captain . . . ?" That single word held a paragraph of worry.

"Sorry, Scotty, I forgot you were on hold. It seems—it seems there's going to be something of a delay here. Dr. McCoy's been arrested and—"

Over the kilometers and through the clouds the chief engineer's astonished yelp cut him off. *"DR. MCCOY ARRESTED?* What for . . . ?"

Kirk tried to frame the word "genocide," found that the effort of linking that concept to McCoy brought him close to blackout.

"Murder," he finally managed to mutter.

"Murder?" Scott paused. When he spoke again, his voice was no longer querulous. "Sir, if you'd like me and some of the security specialists to beam down just in case, I'm sure there'd be no lack of volun . . ."

"Belay that kind of talk, Mr. Scott!" Kirk said, summoning his usual firmness. "The warrant itself appears to be legitimate, issued and authorized by the proper authorities. Mr. Spock and I are going to double-check it now. We're at the local administration building. I'll keep you posted."

"Should I put the ship on alert, sir?"

"No, Mr. Scott. While it may prove hard to restrain natural impulses, this is the time for careful consideration. The Draymians have been scrupulously correct about this. They've made nothing resembling a hostile gesture toward us. And, Scotty, this is not for general dissemination aboard. What I've just told you stays on the Bridge."

"Aye sir," Scott replied quietly.

"Kirk out."

It was all so absurd, Kirk mused, as they moved deeper into the enormous structure. Bones was no more guilty of mass murder than he was of unnecessarily vivisecting a frog. The good doctor was inherently incapable of either maliciousness or incompetence on such a scale.

And yet . . .

There *was* the official warrant, the insane accusation. He stared at the original communication where it was locked behind triple transparent barriers. Despite Demos' and the Prefect's confidence in his willingness to obey his own laws, Kirk found himself having to fight the urge to simply call Scotty to beam them up and out of this treacherous city. Such an action could precipitate an uncomfortable interstellar incident, he knew. The Draymians wouldn't hesitate to publicize it throughout the civilized galaxy. If the Federation didn't adhere to its own laws, why should potential allies be forced to?

He noticed that they had moved into a small office adjoining the well-guarded transmission. Demos sat across from them behind a large desk of white stone. He was answering most of the questions he had expected Kirk to ask.

"Dr. McCoy," the security chief explained, "headed a mass inoculation program against harmful diseases on Dramia II some nineteen of your subjective years ago.

"He was not yet—annointed? No, appointed—a full doctor at the time of this program. Soon after his small medical force departed, a massive plague struck. Fatalities were near total in the growing colony we'd established—established at much expense in life and wealth, Captain Kirk.

"The Dramia II colony constituted our first step away from our home world. Thanks to your Dr. McCoy, the result has been that for the past two decades we have been unable to progress any farther. Since the plague incident public reaction becomes virulent at the mere mention of deep-space exploration or settlement." He looked grim.

"Such has been the result of your *aid*."

"You talk about this plague," Kirk shot back tersely, "as if you were certain Bones was personally responsible for it. Just because it occurred at the same time doesn't mean it was his fault."

Demos leaned forward and displayed front canines. "Believe me, Captain Kirk, we would also like very much to have the rest of the medical team that served under him. However, it appears this is not possible. Therefore we will settle for having the one who was in charge of those responsible for the disaster. It *is* his responsibility, whether directly or otherwise!"

Demos sat back and looked satisfied. "It is enough."

"You talk as if you'd already tried him and found him guilty."

"Captain, you cannot imagine the kind of emotional reaction the mere mention of the Dramia II debacle stirs in the hearts of the people. Feeling runs high even among those who did not have friends or relatives among the dead. It was a . . . a racial disaster. Furthermore, we could not even chance intensive study of the immediate causes lest we risk bringing the plague here,

thus destroying our entire civilization. This has intensified the people's frustration and anger." He glanced
away from Kirk.

"But after all these many years, we still can find no
other possible cause than some carelessness on the part
of Dr. McCoy and his medical team. As to his final
guilt or innocence, the trial will say."

"Trial!" Kirk blurted. "Kangaroo court, you mean.
By your own admission, Bones can hardly expect any-
thing like a fair trial from your people. McCoy is a
Federation citizen and—"

To every one of Kirk's plaints, Demos quietly referred to the copy of the maddening warrant, lying between them on his desk.

"His own government appears to feel that in this
case such rights can properly be waived."

Kirk snorted derisively. "What kind of justice can
Bones expect from a world that accepts our medical
supplies with one hand and imprisons our medical
officer with the other?"

"You are becoming emotional, Captain," Spock ventured.

"Of course I am!" Kirk shouted at his first officer,
while Demos was muttering something about returning
measure for measure.

"Bones harming other beings . . . ," Kirk continued,
"you know better, Spock. Anyone knows better than
that—even those desk-bound morons at Administrative
and Judicial know better."

The captain rambled on as Spock tried to calm him.
Demos studied the two men with some detachment.

Alone—oh, how alone!—and forgotten, the fourth
inhabitant of the tiny office rested his arms on his
thighs and struggled to recall the events of nineteen
years past. He found only hazy memories clouded by
age. So much had happened since, so little had happened then . . .

Dramia II: colony, alien, Advanced Intern McCoy.
His second extrasolar assignment, his first medical
command. Draymia—bustling, alive, thriving. Dramia
II—a bleak, chill world, but promising. Willing giants,
fish-eyed—their nervous children already his own size.

Weeks of boredom, routine, of looking at nothing but alien arms—his crew anxious to move on to another assignment, more challenging, nearer home, with better opportunities for advancement.

Nineteen years. What had those hundreds of inoculations been for? What had been the contents of those ampules? An impurity overlooked, an imperfection in sealing—what? He had known so little then, and now he knew so much. If he could only go back, go back.

"I wish I could be as sure, Jim," a voice vaguely like his own finally murmured.

Conversation in the room died, and with McCoy's words, something inside Kirk died a little, too.

II

At least the cell they put him in was comfortable.

It had no bars, and the larger chamber was no more than normally oppressive, as jails went. The furnishings within the cell were simple, but at least they were sized to McCoy's non-Draymian proportions.

"I just can't be positive," he was mumbling from behind the lightly radiant force-field. He had been talking to himself like that ever since Demos and a patrol of oversized Draymians had escorted him to this forlorn waiting place.

"Is it possible that I somehow was, somehow am responsible for the—"

"Ridiculous!" Kirk objected sharply.

"There is surely," Spock added with his usual assurance, "ample reason to believe that the termination of your inoculation program and the subsequent outbreak of plague on the Dramia II colony is coincidence."

"There's also ample reason to believe that it was a tragic mistake of some kind on my part," McCoy whispered.

"I don't buy that, Bones," Kirk said firmly. "I'm not going to sit around and let someone else sell it to the Federation, either."

"You have something in mind, Captain," Spock responded. It was not a question.

Kirk turned. "A little pretrail investigation, Mr. Spock. A bit of harmless fact gathering—independent fact gathering—to aid Draymian justice." He gestured.

One of the several guards in the chamber moved to the wall, touched a series of switches on a small hand control. The secondary force-field vanished, and Kirk and Spock moved clear. The guard touched another combination and the backup field flamed up again, leaving McCoy totally isolated.

Kirk flipped open his communicator without a backward glance. "Kirk to *Enterprise*—beam us up, Mr. Scott."

"How many, Captain?"

"Two. Just two, Mr. Scott."

"Captain," the chief engineer's voice began, "I think—"

"Beam up, Scotty—now," Kirk repeated.

"Aye, sir."

The twin dissolution that followed was colorful, not destructive. McCoy was left alone in his cell. Well, not entirely alone.

The single guard who remained after Kirk and Spock had departed strolled over and peered curiously at the prisoner. He knew of the Terran's reputed crime. It was an honor to be one of those assigned to watch him, to be one of the few designated to see to his health—so he would be fit and well for the trial.

McCoy did not object to serving as the bug in an alien bottle. He was too depressed to think coherently about anything save his own sudden, shocking change of fortune.

"Your friends may scour the surface of Dramia II to the bedrock," the guard informed the despondent figure within the cage. "They will find nothing to save you. We are a civilized race. Our court system is swift and efficient." In the manner of all jailers, he grinned at his own ironic joke.

As is universally the case with prisoners subjected to such humor, McCoy did not find it amusing.

Words alternated with pictures alternated with charts. Sometimes all three combined on the lab screen to form an especially brilliant and impressive display. The men studying it now were not interested in superficialities, however. They were hunting desperately for a clue to a friend's salvation, and they were not having much luck.

Kirk moved from a small computer annex which was connected to the central computer to stare at the other screen over Spock's shoulder. While Spock was running backward through time, the captain was triple checking the legal fine points of the Federation warrant—to no avail. It was as solid as a warp-drive equation.

"Anything yet, Mr. Spock?"

"No, Captain." The first officer did not turn from the steady flow of information pouring across the screen in front of him. "Our historical records for the Draymian system are few, going back barely two standard decades. Dr. McCoy's medical team was one of the first Federation groups to visit here."

"Kind of unusual, isn't it—for a medical team to be called into a new system so soon after initial contact is opened?"

"Yes, Captain. But apparently the Draymian need was considerable. Understandably Starfleet felt that if we did not respond to their request for assistance, someone else might be only too happy to oblige. The Klingons, for example."

"Granted," Kirk admitted. As usual, Spock's assessment of the situation was infallible.

"Most of the information available on early Federation contact with the Draymians comes from the technical survey teams—planetary and solar data, geophysical statistics—the usual enormous mass of pure information which takes many years to properly integrate and codify for easy computer retrieval."

Abruptly the rapid stream of lines and words froze on screen. Spock pressed another switch and several significant paragraphs blossomed into easily readable lines.

DRAMIA II, LOCAL COLONIZATION, HISTORY OF.

"It's about time," Kirk muttered.

The two officers ran through a mass of detail until they came to: *Plague, Dramia II, colony of Draymia. Origin unknown, characterized by pigmentation shift in skin of victim, debilitation, followed by the onset of terminal coma. Theoretically can affect several species of humanoid including man, quorman, and others.*

Those dead from exposure included corpsman Micheau Pochenko, anesthesiologist Severin Alonzo Hart.

Spock glanced back at Kirk. "It appears that two of Dr. McCoy's own team also died from the plague. Our Draymian hosts neglected to mention that. *Certain species,*" he read, turning back to the screen, "*believed to be naturally immune, notably Tauran and Vulcan.* Interesting."

"Go on, Mr. Spock," Kirk prompted, ignoring the parade of legalese across his own, now unwatched screen . . .

Done with taunting the unresponsive prisoner, the guard reported to Demos what he'd overheard when the murderer had spoken with his two superiors.

"You are certain?"

"Yes, my commander," the guard insisted stiffly. "The Federation Captain is planning to visit Dramia II to gather material negative to our case against human filth, McCoy."

"Thank you, guard. Speak of this to no one else, please. You may leave."

"It shall be as you desire, Commander." The guard saluted and left.

Demos sat thinking for several minutes. There was no telling what distortion of truth the clever Federation officers might glean from the poor, blighted ruin of Dramia II. But the people of Draymia had waited stoically for their revenge these past years. He, Demos, was not about to see them deprived of it. Whatever tricks, whatever perversion of logic Captain Kirk could concoct from the ruined colony must not go unobserved. And this was not something he could trust to underlings.

He activated a switch within the bonelike mass of the desk, a switch that didn't appear to exist.

"Ready my personal skiff immediately . . ."

Kirk was aware he was proceeding without proper authority. But he wasn't about to contact Starfleet for permission—after all, that *proper authority* had issued the damning warrant in the first place. They could call

him on the deck afterward—after he had proven
Bones' innocence.

"Estimated time of arrival, Mr. Sulu?"

Sulu checked a readout, reported, "Four hours ship
time, sir."

"Move it up a little if the computer can handle the
acceleration compensation. The Draymians will *probably* stick to their normal courtroom procedure.
However, this is a special case to them, and they may
be interested in rushing it to completion. Also, we've
no idea how long it may take us to turn up proof of
Bones' innocence.

"Demos, their security chief, emphasized the civilized nature of his people. But if it becomes public information that the government is now holding the
being they consider responsible for the extinction of
their sole off-planet colony, I wouldn't be surprised to
see a spirit of vigilantism take over."

"Do not confuse human and alien motivation, Captain," advised Spock.

"I wish that were a uniquely human tendency, Mr.
Spock. Unfortunately, it appears from stellar history
that we've no monopoly on mob law."

"Unfortunate, indeed, Captain."

Spock's observation had ramifications that Kirk
would have liked to pursue but the captain's thoughts
were interrupted by a call from the helm.

"Ship in pursuit, Captain."

"Origin?"

Sulu hurriedly checked sensors. "Undoubtedly from
Draymia, sir. I'm running the recorder back—here it
is, no bigger than a two-man scout."

"Full magnification of the aft screen."

"I'm on full, sir."

Kirk squinted at the screen, which showed only distant stars. "I don't see anything, Mr. Sulu."

"No, sir. Sensors had it for only a moment. The ship
apparently was following just out of maximum scanner
range. When we suddenly increased our speed, its pilot
jumped to stay with us and for a second or two, over-
compensated. He's dropped back out of detector range
again."

"But not transmission range," Uhura observed. "Shall I attempt contact, Captain?"

"No, Lieutenant, not just yet."

"May I inquire as to the reason?" This from a curious Spock.

"We seem to have two choices, Mr. Spock. We can let this busybody—who is obviously out to make things difficult for us, else he wouldn't be skulking about our stern—continue to think he's succeeding at his game. Or we can try to make things easier for him."

"Easier, Captain? I fail to understand."

"He could certainly cause us more trouble at a crucial moment by sneaking aboard. That would be simple for him to do, since we've carelessly left open the doors to the Shuttlecraft Bay."

"Captain, the doors aren't open," Uhura pointed out.

"Oh, yes—take care of that little undersight, will you, Mr. Sulu? Mr. Spock, issue a general order—all internal lights near exterior ports, all observation lounge illumination, to be extinguished.

"As far as I know, no Draymian has ever been aboard a Federation cruiser while it was in transit. They know as little about us as we do about them. I'd like to give the impression that most of the crew is off-duty, asleep."

"Anyone approaching would assume we still have automatic detectors operational, Captain."

"Any representative of a seasoned space-traveling race would, Mr. Spock. But the Draymians are new at this. Besides, we've already given in to their demands to hand over Bones. Why would we have defensive screens up within their system, when we've already shown we abide by the law?

"Whoever's back there is convinced he's eluded us so far. Let's at least give him the opportunity to elude us a little farther . . ."

The lights went out aboard the great starship. On board his small skiff, Demos saw them fade.

He only had suppositions about Federation habits with which to judge the situation, but there had been no sign from the cruiser that his presence had been de-

tected yet. If it had, he couldn't understand not receiving at least a querulous hail. So the decision he
reached was precisely the one Kirk was hoping he
would.

He edged his tiny vessel ahead—slowly at first, then,
as silence continued, with increasing confidence. If the
big ship's hangar doors were not automatic, he would
be forced to use a suit.

The skiff slid silently into the cavernous hold and
settled to a stop. Atmospheric considerations vanished
when the hangar doors closed behind him and gauges
monitored the rise of air pressure outside. The hold
was empty of personnel, but not of concealment.
Demos slipped his craft between two others, concealing
it from all but direct view. In size and shape it did not
differ enough from a Federation scout to immediately
catch the attention of some idly strolling crew member.
Of course, these were all rationalizations. But the
chance to actually inspect the inner workings of a Federation battle cruiser was too tempting to Demos' martial mentality for him to pass by.

Let him have two time-parts . . . one even . . .

He found the door leading to the first access corridor
and peered cautiously through the transparent port set
in its upper third. The passageway beyond was
deserted. Opening the door and stooping slightly to
avoid the overhead arch, he made his way into the
empty main corridor.

If he could just find someplace to secrete himself for
a while till he got his bearings . . .

The next doorway had no port. He would have to
take a chance. The opening mechanism was clearly
marked and easily operated. He activated it and the
door slid aside.

Reflexively, he reached for the weapon at his belt.

"Not now, Demos, you're hardly in a position to
take on the entire crew," Kirk murmured evenly.

The hand dipping toward the gun relaxed, continued
smoothly onwards to scratch at an imaginary itch on
his leg.

"And you," he countered with a touch of impatience, "are not in authority to conduct an investigation in this system."

Kirk's tone was conciliatory as he turned to his first officer. "You will remind me to report my unbecoming attitude to the Federation, won't you, Spock?"

"Of course, Captain."

"I demand you report to your superiors now, and that I be permitted to sit in on—"

"Actually, Demos," Kirk interrupted, "you're hardly in a position to demand much of anything. But I'll surprise you, I think, by saying that I'll happily oblige. Unfortunately, we're out of communications range with Starfleet Central at the moment."

"Report to the nearest Starbase, then—"

"Sorry, you asked me to report to my *superiors*. By your own admission, exceeding our authority to conduct this type of investigation is a matter for consideration at the highest levels. And I wouldn't *think* of insulting you by laying the matter before some minor functionary."

"Then, I myself will proceed to your Starbase and report this violation for you." Demos turned and started back down the corridor, feeling strangely flat eyes on the back of his head.

"I'm afraid your ship has been impounded, Commander, for your own protection."

Demos whirled, furious. "My own protec—"

"You'd never reach Starbase with it."

"So *you* say," Demos muttered angrily. "Just as you say you are out of communications range with your Central Headquarters."

"Yes, and there's something else I say," Kirk went on, now even more firmly.

"You are a stowaway, Commander," Spock informed the angry security chief. "You are in violation, I believe, of one of your own laws."

Demos started to say something, but his words became tangled as a sudden realization of his situation set in. "You planned it . . . you planned this so that it would appear legal, so that my abduction would not seem to break any laws."

"We merely offered you the chance to realize your

own desires, Demos," Kirk replied firmly. "I seem to recall a similar course of action recently taken against a Federation citizen by your own government. You wouldn't happen to remember the name of that unlucky individual, would you? His name was McCoy, Leonard McCoy. Maybe now you can sympathize with his situation a little more, Commander. In fact, I'd think you'd begin to acquire a personal interest in it."

"I have a personal interest in seeing justice done," Demos snapped, drawing himself up.

"Excellent." Kirk turned to leave. "Mr. Spock, see to the Commander's comfort. It's good to hear he's after the same thing we are . . ."

Dramia II loomed on the screen before them, a brown and red crescent splotched only fitfully with greens and blues. A harsh-looking world on which to try to mold a new civilization.

The Draymians had been courageous enough to try. They had been rewarded with death and desolation.

Ironically, the vacuum surrounding that stark planet blazed with beauty. Dramia II swam in the midst of one of the massive deep-space auroras for which the Dramian system had first been noted. Brilliant reds, purples, and blues glowed under powerful bombardment from Dramia's sun, forming a fiery curtain in space. Several shifting, metallic streamers draped themselves across the planet, masking portions of it with ionized glory.

"Lovely phenomenon."

"Yes, Captain," Spock agreed. "According to records, it is one of several such scattered through the system. It was the highlight of the first Federation survey here." He nodded toward the screen.

"This band of particulate matter is the farthest out from the sun itself."

"I see. Surface radiation level, Mr. Sulu?"

"Still working on it, Captain."

A moment, then, "I see the figures," Spock reported. "The level is strong, but nowhere lethal. There *are* some as yet unclassifiable aspects to the readings obtained where one of the auroral streamers intersects the atmosphere of Dramia II, which—"

Kirk cut him short. "We'll have time for research after we secure Dr. McCoy's release."

"Yes, Captain."

Nearby, Demos made a derisive sound.

"All I'm concerned about is that it's safe for us to
beam down," Kirk continued. "Since it appears to be
... shall we, gentlemen?" He rose from the command
chair and started for the elevator door, followed by
Spock and Demos.

Scott was waiting for them in the transporter room.
He voiced his own concerns immediately.

"Are you sure it's safe, Captain?"

"As safe as our sensors are sure, Scotty.
Absolutely."

"Not absolutely, Captain. Our sensing equipment is
never absolutely sure," Spock corrected.

Kirk grinned, looked over at Demos who was studying the transporter alcove with what seemed like momentary hesitation.

"Mr. Spock, you're not trying to scare our Draymian
comrade, are you? You can still remain aboard if you
wish, Commander."

The Draymian chief of security stared evenly back at
him. "I came to make certain you fabricated no intricate lies, Captain Kirk. I go."

He stepped up into the transporter and assumed a
somewhat cramped pose of readiness.

"You heard him, Mr. Scott. Energize."

Scott looked unhappy, but set about the familiar operation. He adjusted the necessary switches, pulled the
requisite levers. There was the familiar whine of
complaining atoms, and the three figures were gone ...

Three pillars of shattered crystal solidified on the
sandy surface and shaped themselves into upright containers of intelligence.

Kirk stumbled slightly on rematerialization—the surface underfoot was loose and windblown. Part of the
region they had set down in was still verdant. Trees
and hedgerows of Draymian flora had been planted
here.

But the irrigation systems had broken down under
nineteen years of neglect. The desert had encroached

ever more boldly on what had once been the fertile periphery of the two colony towns.

Around them lay the battered, partially decomposed remains of homes and warehouses and offices—evidence of angry winds, of sand pitted against walls. Dunes were piled up to the sills of windows devoid of glass, which stared with vacant sockets at the advancing drifts.

Here and there were signs of old fires. Kirk hoped they had been caused by natural means and not by the last vestiges of isolated, panicked sentience. Reversion from civilization to barbarism in a single generation was never very pretty, no matter which world was involved.

The physical detritus was sobering. He could imagine what that final, plague-rotted collapse must have been like. Still, it was one thing to imagine and quite another to stand in the midst of such imaginings. His quota of sympathy for the Draymians went up another notch, though the sight of this graveyard of hopes did nothing to shake his confidence in McCoy's innocence.

"Not the most enchanting scene I've ever beheld," he finally murmured.

"Plague seldom leaves behind fields of flowers and dancing children, Captain."

Kirk glared angrily at the security chief, who simply stared over the Captain's head with the serene gaze of the self-righteous. Spock raised an eyebrow.

"There must have been local medical facilities—one central hospital, at least. I would assume they are less severely damaged than these structures here, as logic dictates they would be the last buildings to be abandoned. It would be a good place to begin our search."

Again, Demos made that strange Draymian shrug. "As you wish. This is so hopeless. Why not depart our system in peace, now, and leave destiny to take its inevitable course?"

"I'm afraid," Kirk said tightly, "that inevitable is a word I'm not familiar with. If you could direct us . . . ?"

Demos turned and pointed toward a slightly higher cluster of ruins lying near the approximate center of the first town.

"That must be what remains of the communications station. According to Draymian town plan, the medical facilities should have been built several blocks further north and a little to the east."

Kirk nodded curtly, and they slogged off through thick sand in the indicated direction. Soon after they started their progress improved as the clinging sand gave way to pockmarked but still serviceable pavement.

They were in the outskirts of the town proper when they noticed something moving on their right—moving sharply and jerkily; it was neither subtle nor inconspicuous. All three marchers saw it. Surprisingly, it was Demos who looked fearful while they surveyed the rubble.

"Some danger?" Kirk wondered. Demos' eyes studied the rim of the debris with practiced skill.

"If you remember, Captain Kirk, I said that *nearly* everyone on Dramia II was killed. There were reports of some survivors by later survey crews—which did not touch down, of course. I think 'survivors' is an overly optimistic classification for any pitiful souls forever marooned here.

"One drone was sent down some eight years ago. It was at that time that these survivors acquired a reputation for not liking outsiders."

"Hardly surprising," Spock commented, "in view of what they must feel. They could not be expected to act logically. But surely you cannot be considered an outsider, Commander. You are as Draymian as they. I should think the sight of a fellow being would fill them with pleasure."

"The sight of a fellow *Draymian* might," Demos replied, with a bitter half-chuckle. "But there are no Draymians left on this world . . . not as we know them. The gulf between us now is that which separates the living and the walking dead."

There was more movement to the far right of the crumbled wall they were watching. Kirk would never have noticed it had he not been looking idly at that exact spot when the figure decided to abandon the area.

"Walking dead he may be but he still has some spirit left in him. He mustn't get away!"

Kirk started on the run after the retreating biped. Spock moved up quickly alongside. Demos hesitated for several long seconds. Apparently deciding it would be better to go along than remain alone in the open street, he raced after them. Enormous strides quickly caught him up to the two smaller men.

Had the figure been healthy it undoubtedly could have lost its pursuers easily in the maze of tumbling walls and hollowed-out structures. The few glances they had of it showed it to be ragged and hunched. It ran with a peculiar loping gait.

"There, Captain," Spock husked, "it went around that mound."

The mound had once served as the foundation for a higher, silo-like building. Now it was all crumbled in on itself, a concrete caldera. Sharp-edged blocks of broken masonry protruded here and there from the circular heap.

They rounded the hillock—and came to a sudden halt on the other side. The pavement here was open for several meters in every direction, save where the furrowed brow of a cliff-faced hill backed into the town. There were no structures, tumbled or otherwise, that their limping quarry could have reached in time to conceal himself before they had rounded the ruin.

"I was afraid of that," Kirk panted. "He's got some secret cubbyhole he's slipped into. Almost looks like someone pulled him out with a transporter."

"Hardly likely, Captain," Spock observed drily. He moved toward the cliff-face while Demos and Kirk stood surveying the nearest ruins.

"I believe your initial supposition was correct, Captain," Spock soon called to them. They walked over to where he stood, staring into a vertical slit in the naked stone.

The crevice wasn't wide, but by turning sideways and holding his breath, a Draymian could squeeze through. It would be easier for Kirk and Spock.

Spreading out as far as possible to cover one another, the two officers from the *Enterprise* approached the opening. Nothing inorganic and unpleasant issued to meet them.

They started in. It grew darker ... and then it didn't.

"Light inside," Kirk murmured softly. "Can't be a cave, then."

"Possibly one whose roof has collapsed wholly or partially," his first officer theorized. They continued to edge forward, hugging the cold rock wall. A grainy tenor sounded behind them.

"I would advise against this, Captain," Demos said. "Dramia II is little visited. We have no idea what kind of mutations the plague may have spawned among the local life-forms, of which several ..."

"Save the biology lecture, Demos. You won't mind if I ignore your advice."

"Extreme caution in this restricted area would seem advisable, Captain."

"I'll watch myself, Spock, but I'm not going to lose that survivor. There may not be any others nearby, and we haven't much time. Also, if this one escapes, he may warn others of our presence. We may never spot another one."

The captain moved forward steadily, trying to make as little noise on the gravel underfoot as possible. "Bones' life is on the line, Mr. Spock. I don't mind taking a few risks."

The light dimmed until it was almost dark, but it never died entirely. Ahead he could detect patches of brightness. A few more steps, and Kirk emerged into a broad chamber.

Spock had been right. They stood in a cave whose ceiling had collapsed in places. The floor was dotted with mounds of fallen roof. He looked around, but there was no sign of their quarry.

Water waxed the rock dark and shiny where it issued in a steady trickle from cracks in a rock face. The tiny rivulets formed a small pool. Shade from the desert sun, protection from unrestricted carnivores, and water. His senses sharpened—this *had* to be their limping refugee's home. Kirk hoped they hadn't scared him out of it.

"Captain ... are you all right?" Kirk snapped back

to wakefulness, aware that Spock and Demos were waiting for his okay to proceed.

"All clear, Mr. Spock, come ahead." Kirk walked to the edge of the pool, nudged a pile of charred wood with his foot. "Cave dwellers," he muttered, "in a civilization as high as Draymia's."

"The result of your Dr. McCoy and his *civilized* medicine," the security chief responded coldly. Kirk whirled.

"Look, Demos, I'm getting a mite sick of your steady accusations. Until you can prove—"

A shadow suddenly detached itself from its dark companions and flung itself forward. It was no less gargoylish in form than its inorganic brothers.

At one time it had doubtless been intelligent—an intelligence now transcended by the madness shining in its eyes. It landed just behind Kirk, knocking him to the ground, and began flailing at him in frantic, howling anguish.

Momentarily stunned, Kirk couldn't dislodge his assailant, because of the latter's sheer bulk and unthinking rage. Fortunately, the same blind fury that drove the pitiable specimen to attack Kirk saved the captain from any serious harm, for the Draymian struck aimlessly, with neither skill nor design. Thus Kirk was able to shield himself from all the wild blows until Spock and Demos could wrestle the hysterical figure away.

The captain rolled over, his only injury a lack of breath.

"Captain . . ."

"Okay, Spock . . . I'm okay. He *wanted* to hurt me more than he actually did."

"And why do you think he attacked you, Captain?" asked Demos, struggling to restrain the gradually subsiding madman.

Kirk got to his feet, spoke slowly. "I was the nearest to his hiding place." Demos indicated the negative.

"You are also the only human among us, Captain Kirk. Don't attempt to evade the obvious. You were attacked because you are human—as is Dr. McCoy."

Damn you, Demos, Kirk cried silently. *And damn this whole insane system.* But he said nothing, merely dusted his uniform and moved to study the captive.

Fear had been replaced on the latter's face by re-
morse, anger by sorrow and misery; and that initial cry
of fury became an utterly heart-rending whimper.
Clearly the creature was no longer a threat.

"Let him go," Kirk whispered.

"Are you sure, Captain?" Spock asked.

Kirk stared into the captive's eyes. They didn't meet
his own. Instead they were focused on some other,
greater horror now—one too distant to encompass the
three figures around him.

Cautiously, Demos and Spock turned Kirk's assailant
loose. That tortured soul turned, took two steps, and
fell to his knees. He dropped onto his side and just lay
there, moaning and sobbing uncontrollably.

Now Kirk knew they had to find *absolute,* incontro-
vertible proof that Bones was innocent. Supposition and
verbal reasoning were not going to sway the decision of
people who had been subjected to reports of this kind
of emotional and mental destruction.

Nevertheless, he couldn't keep from voicing the inner certainty that kept him going.

"Demos, you've got to believe me. Dr. McCoy could
never be responsible for something like . . . like that."
He gestured to where the insane being gibbered mind-
lessly on the stone floor.

"Good intentions cannot wipe out the existence of
evil results, Captain."

"But how did this one survive the plague?" Kirk
wondered aloud, when an especially tortured howl rose
from the no-longer-dangerous survivor.

Demos explained. "He and a few others were away,
on the home world and elsewhere, when the plague
struck. They returned before they could be stopped, to
find everyone they'd known—loved ones, companions,
everyone—dead of the plague.

"They chose to remain, to live here in the home they
had once known." The security chief's voice was close
to cracking. "Nineteen years of grief—there are worse
plagues than those caused by germs. You see now,
Captain Kirk, there were no actual survivors on
Dramia II.

III

"I *thought* I heard sounds of fighting, and voices!"

The words that penetrated to the startled listeners were clear and strong, ringing loud in the cave.

"You're wrong, whoever you are," it continued. "There was at least one survivor."

A tall Draymian was walking toward them, climbing over a rocky hillock formed by part of the fallen ceiling. His clothes were ragged, his countenance worn, but otherwise he resembled Demos far more than he did the twisted figure rolling about on the cave floor.

"I was not found by any of the observation parties, nor by the crews of those ships which came to leave the mourners here. But I survived the plague—by what miracle I do not know. I'd given up hope of ever being rescued."

"You must remember what it was like, then," Kirk began excitedly. "During the plague ... you can tell us."

"I remember," the newcomer nodded, oblivious to Demos' unbelieving stare. "I remember the people around me, even the doctors, turning blue, then green, and finally a dull red color, collapsing, strength ebbing, then ..."

He stopped, his strong voice fading, the last softly whispered words echoing down hidden pathways in the cave.

"The pigmentation changes associated with the disease, as mentioned in the records, Captain," Spock commented.

Kirk nodded quickly, keeping his attention focused

on the survivor. "You *must* remember," he asked anxiously, "before the plague struck, there was a visiting mission here from the Federation, a medical mission that included humans among its personnel.

"They were led by a man named McCoy—Dr. Leonard McCoy. He was responsible for seeing to the vaccination of the entire colony. He must have treated you too ... or at least overseen your treatment. *Do you remember him?*"

Kirk had no idea what to expect from the long-isolated alien, surviving amidst the ruins of a forgotten colony and its unstable inhabitants. Some hesitation, surely—a first imperfect attempt at resurrecting a faint memory of a distasteful past.

Instead, the survivor brightened immediately and spoke as though he were talking of yesterday.

"A Terran physician, young—of course, I remember Dr. McCoy. How could I forget the being who saved my life?"

Despite social and physical interspecies differences, the glances that passed then among Kirk, Demos and Spock needed no interpretation.

"Then that is also the man," Demos finally declared, "who is responsible for the death of this colony." And he waved at the surrounding desolation.

The survivor was neither intimidated nor impressed —as one might expect of a being who had successfully survived among the corpses of thousands, living and dead. He stared evenly back at the Commander of Draymian security.

"We knew little of the Federation and its various races, those many years ago," he began slowly. "It has been a long time. Perhaps we know more of them now. But I believe that even those many triads ago we knew that the differences between us were not great.

"Although I knew this Dr. McCoy very briefly, I think I came to know him well. I cannot believe you are speaking of the same person who saved my life." The survivor looked thoughtful, reminiscing.

"At times he appeared less than positive, yes, and sometimes gave the impression of hesitation. But he did everything with a kindness and concern for the afflicted that was honest. You, Commander whoever-you-are . . ."

"Demos, of Draymian Internal Security."

"Well, Demos, Commander of Draymian Security, I, Kolti, think you have the wrong man," he concluded firmly. "One who saves does not also murder."

Demos threw Kolti a stare of frustration and anger; but the survivor had seen far worse things these past years than the gaze of the overbearing security chief. He gave no sign of altering his story or his regard for Dr. McCoy.

A smile had replaced Kirk's concerned stare. Spock's eyebrows ascended as the captain inquired, "So you're certain it was this Dr. McCoy who saved you?"

"Indeed, this is so."

"It's been several lifetimes for you, Kolti," Kirk observed, eyeing the tall Draymian appraisingly, "and I know you're anxious to be home."

"I've outgrown impatience," Kolti told them softly.

"You look like the sort of intelligent being who would place certain things above personal comfort. You've heard what your security chief says. Dr. McCoy saved your life. Not many have an opportunity to repay such a debt. You do.

"Will you delay your return to friends and family long enough to help clear his name and prevent a permanent stain from entering the annals of Draymian justice?"

"I would not be here to be offered the choice were it not for your Dr. McCoy. I will do whatever you ask of me."

Kirk nodded. He had his proof . . . committed proof, from a source which could neither be argued with nor intimidated. He pulled out the communicator.

"Mr. Scott . . . beam us aboard, all four of us. And quickly—we may have spent too much time here already."

"Aye aye, sir," came the chief engineer's enthusiastic response.

Near the back of the cavern, by broken shards of

limestone and shale, a rocking, moaning figure suddenly rolled upright and ceased its whimpers as the miracle took place before its eyes. Fragments of the sun appeared and swallowed up the four figures.

It was over quickly. Then he was alone in his cave again with the nearby water and approaching night . . .

Kirk was stepping down from the alcove and speaking as soon as full reintegration finished.

"Get me the Bridge, Mr. Scott." Scott activated the transporter console intercom, stepped aside as Kirk took up station behind it.

"Sulu, Arex, get under way immediately. Back to Draymia, at top intersystem speed."

Acknowledgment came back over the speaker, and Kirk clicked off, then saw Scott staring at the ragged but unbent Kolti.

"I know you told me to beam up four, and four I beamed up, Captain. But, who is *that?*"

"A Dramian friend of Dr. McCoy's."

"A *Dramian* friend . . . ?"

Scott broke off in astonishment but continued to gaze open-mouthed at Kolti. The survivor stepped gingerly from the transporter alcove and stared in amazement around him. Scott walked around the console and extended a hand to the bemused alien.

"I don't know where you've been hiding yourself, laddie, but somehow I get the feelin' you've got to be a clan member in good standin'. What's your tartan like?"

"Clan member . . . tartan?" Kolti wondered aloud as Kirk and Spock conducted him toward the turbolift, with Demos trailing along.

"Merely Mr. Scott's way of saying that we find in you a kindred spirit which heretofore has seemed lacking in your people." Spock turned pensive. "We may still be too late to save Dr. McCoy. Even if we are not, your testimony may not be enough to shift the tide of feeling which has been raised against him. But there is historical precedent—instances where the courage of one has been enough to overcome the reckless emotionalism of many."

"Spock's trying to say," Kirk explained tautly, "that we think you've got the guts to go through with this." He waved off Kolti's reply. "Be modest later, after we've saved McCoy. For now, Mr. Spock, conduct Kolti to Sick Bay. Have Nurse Chapel check him out completely. Pull everything we've got on Draymian medicine. And see that he has anything he wants."

"I would settle, Captain Kirk," Kolti murmured, "for some food and a clean bed."

Kirk nodded, turned back to Scott. "I want you to push the navigation computer, Scotty. Get us to Draymia as fast as posible—overshoot, if necessary. Minutes may count. The Draymians," he finished, glancing up at Demos, "are impatient for their revenge."

"Most assuredly," the security chief confirmed.

"I'll pour on the coal, Captain," Scott grinned.

They were ten minutes out from Dramia II and nearing Draymia when Kirk finally relaxed from the hysteria of last-minute emergency preparations long enough to check with Sick Bay.

"Mr. Spock, are you still with our patient?"

"Affirmative, Captain," the calm voice came back.

"How's he doing?"

"A moment, Captain . . ." Spock glanced back to where Kolti was sleeping the sleep of the exhausted in the infirmary bed behind him.

Only Spock had noticed how utterly fatigued their passenger was. He had gone along with the other's pose, admiring the silent fortitude as he had answered questions for both Kirk and then Chapel. As was the case with most sophonts, his expression was far more truthful in sleep.

Chapel hurried past him, to adjust the makeshift instrumentation rigged over the slumberer's bed.

"He appears to be in reasonably good health though terribly debilitated and worn out. At the moment he is resting quietly. A brave man, Captain."

"Brave enough to be the unimpeachable witness we need, I hope," Kirk replied. He glanced up at the main viewscreen. Their truncated course was taking them through the body of one of the magnificent intersystem auroras. "Let's hope the trial hasn't already begun."

Sulu spoke to him. "Approaching Draymia orbit, sir."

"You heard, Spock? I think we can get Demos to beam down to put a hold on the proceedings long enough until our witness is fit to appear before a legal assemblage and to answer questions."

"The trial may be academic, Captain."

Kirk sat straighter in his chair. Spock's voice had abruptly taken on a new tone, even as always but touched now with a faint twinge of . . . worry?

"What's the trouble, Mr. Spock?"

At the other end of the comm, the *Enterprise*'s first officer was once more studying the sleeping Kolti. The survivor of Dramia II still rested quietly . . . but the expression on his face was no longer content. Nor was that the most noticeable change in his features.

"Captain, Kolti is turning blue."

Very blue. Normally a creamy chalcedony in color, the alien's skin had shifted to a pale shade of cerulean. The color shift might have seemed amusing to some, at worst worrying. But the implications were neither of a humorous nor of a mildly upsetting nature. The implications were deadly.

Especially for one Leonard McCoy, M.D., USSIT

Kirk touched the switch and the door dilated, admitting him to Sick Bay. Followed closely by Spock and Demos, he rushed to the quarantine chamber where Kolti had been isolated hurriedly. Chapel was at the Draymian's bedside, taking readings with a modified medical tricorder.

"I'm sorry, Captain," she finally said. "Everything correlates with the readings the built-ins give. I have no idea what . . ."

"Plague!" Demos gasped after only a quick glance at the prone Draymian.

Kirk spun on the security chief. If there was any foul play at work here, any attempt to offer up McCoy as scapegoat by eliminating his only convincing witness . . . His suspicions were dulled by two things—the fear in the commander's voice and the expression on his face. Not even a master Draymian thespian, he suspected, could have managed to conjure up a look of such pure terror.

"Seal off this entire infirmary, Lieutenant Chapel. No one else is to be admitted, no one is to leave." Chapel darted to the nearest intercom to issue the requisite order, all the while working with the recalibrated tricorder.

Spock was bent over the motionless form of Kolti. "I know little Draymian physiology, Captain, and even less of their reactions to specific diseases. But consider that Kolti has been through nearly twenty of our years of extreme privation. When brought aboard he was weak, undernourished and on the verge of physical collapse.

"Now . . . this. Plague or not, he is no longer in a condition to submit testimony at any kind of trial."

"We've got to save him," Kirk added quietly.

Demos smirked. "For McCoy's sake."

"Yes, for McCoy's sake!" Kirk shot back angrily. "And for Kolti's sake, too." He stood close to the Draymian officer and stared up at the towering biped, for all the world like a terrier challenging a mastiff.

"You see, Commander, we place considerable value on lives other than our own. Does that shock you?"

Demos was suddenly tongue-tied. Kirk's reaction had been unexpectedly violent. Or maybe it was the human's smaller size and controlled politeness which had deceived him till now. He could only begin to stammer, "It is not that . . ."

His jaw dropped and his pop-eyes bulged frighteningly.

Kirk studied him curiously. Surely the brief outburst couldn't have stunned him *this* much.

"Captain . . ." There was something in Spock's voice . . .

Kirk wasn't sure where the impulse originated, but he had a sudden urge to look down at himself. He held up his hands, then slowly turned them over. The palms were blue. Recently examined records welled up in his mind.

Certain species, such as Tauran and Vulcan, are immune. Others . . . The thought died away as he finished, to himself, ". . . such as human, are . . . not."

"Chapel . . . Lieutenant Chapel . . ." He was walking with increasingly rapid steps towards the door leading to the head nurse's office.

She was there . . . sprawled across her desk and turning a rich hue of azure even as he stared.

"Mr. Scott, Chief Kyle, others exposed—quarantine too late," he called back to Spock . . . even as his lower leg muscles turned to water and he slumped to his knees.

Demos weakly reached out a hand to catch him. The Draymian Commander had become sky-colored. Kirk muttered, his head swimming.

"Vulcan immunity! Mr. Spock, take . . . take command." He tried to add something else; but though his mouth moved, no words came forth.

Spock caught him before he collapsed completely. He carried Kirk to an empty bed, then went back and transferred Chapel. He tried to do likewise for the massive Demos; but the Draymian commander's bulk defeated him, and he had no time to wrestle with the huge form. He settled for making Demos as comfortable as possible on the infirmary floor.

Two things must be done immediately—depending on the condition of the crew. It was not good. As Spock made his way toward the bridge, he saw other crew members sprawled where they had fallen, with still-healthy companions trying to aid them. Quarantine appeared to be out of the question. This mysterious affliction spread too fast.

It took hold with alarming speed, the effects irresistible and overwhelming. He ordered the healthy crew members to make the ill as comfortable as possible right where they were found, and then to return to their own posts to continue functioning as long as they were able. It was a brutal, unavoidable order to have to give.

No one argued, no one objected. After all, this was the *Enterprise*.

The situation was no better on the Bridge. Only Sulu still retained anything like his normal color. But even he was showing signs of initial blueness. He did manage to aid Spock in placing the ship into proper orbit around Draymia.

Posterity came next, before survival. He assumed Kirk's seat and activated the recorder.

"Captain's Log, supplemental. First Officer Spock in command, recording.

"We are in orbit around the planet Draymia under conditions of general quarantine. The situation is critical. We have apparently contracted the plague which wiped out the Draymian colony on Dramia II. Nearly the entire ship's complement has already been affected, some seriously.

"A few have shown slightly stronger resistance than others, but this appears transitory. As Acting Commanding Officer, I have ordered the activation of General Order Six." Spock paused, looked over to where Sulu was turning a deep blue color.

"Has the General Order been engaged, Lieutenant?"

"Yes ... sir," the helmsman replied, painfully, slowly.

"If everyone on board has perished or been rendered incapable of action at the end of a twenty-four-hour period," Spock continued, "and the computer has not been contacted with proper authority to cancel, the ship will self-destruct in order to protect other beings from the disease."

As he completed the entry—the last entry, perhaps—he reflected on the irony of the situation. It seemed that Dr. McCoy might outlive them all.

"Interesting," he whispered.

"What, sir?" asked Sulu.

"Report to Sick Bay, Lieutenant.

Sulu's voice was growing thick, unintelligible. "But sir ... you need someone ... to monitor ... to ..."

"I gave you an order, Mr. Sulu. I will ... manage the necessary instrumentation.

Too weak to reply, Sulu got shakily to his feet and started for the elevator. The doors slid apart before he could reach the switch.

Kirk stood there, swaying slightly, but apparently alert and in control of himself. Every step as he moved forward was painful, every shift of an eye felt like the blow of a hammer on his orbicular nerves.

"Spock . . ." he succeeded in whispering.

The first officer whirled, showing as close to an expression of alarm as he was capable of. "Captain, how . . . ? In your condition, it shouldn't be—"

"Stimulants," Kirk muttered. "Pumped full . . . temporary . . ." Spock was at his side, helping him to his command chair. Kirk brushed aside his objections. "Have to find an antidote . . . fast. Only one man . . . maybe. McCoy."

"Captain," Spock countered gently, "the entire medical staff of an advanced world like Draymia could not find an answer to this plague in many years of research."

"We don't know that they applied themselves directly to the problem, Spock. Demos told us how fearful of contamination their observer teams were." His expression twisted. "Whereas Bones always liked to get right into a problem.

"I'd guess the Draymians' quarantine extended to medical personnel too, as soon as they found the plague was one hundred percent fatal. Maybe a few physicians sacrificed themselves trying to find an answer. At the beginning. But even then, they didn't have the advantage of a Federation medical library computer, or a researcher with Bones' skill and experience in dealing with rare diseases.

"We've got to get him back here . . . back here . . ."

"The Draymians will not permit . . ." Spock started to say. He stopped.

Kirk had lapsed into semiconsciousness.

Spock sat thoughtfully, weighing this possibility against that solution, juxtaposing alternatives with probabilities, before eventually making his way to Uhura's vacated communications station.

"Draymia Port," the visage that appeared on the main screen announced.

"This is the Federation starship *Enterprise,* First Officer Spock. I must speak *immediately* with the Supreme Prefect."

"We know of your power and capabilities, Officer

Spock," the figure at the other end said, "but do you think that the Supreme Prefect is a personage who can be called up at every—"

"If I do not speak with the Supreme Prefect instantly," Spock informed the other, "I predict with ninety-seven point eight percent surety the advancement of your status in a backward direction. This matter concerns the Dramia II plague."

Bulging eyes rolled and the communicator began shouting off-screen demands, as the Draymian worked his hands in a series of furious gestures.

The screen flickered. For a moment abstract electronic images danced across the face, then the static cleared and the face of the Supreme Prefect hastily appeared. He was wrestling with his tunic and his dignity as the focus sharpened.

"Mr. Spock, what is the meaning of this? What is this about the plague—and why do you speak and not your captain?"

"Captain Kirk and the majority of the ship's complement are presently incapacitated," Spock answered smoothly. "The Dramia II plague has struck the ship."

"Plague aboard." The Prefect assumed a look of panic. "Surely, Mr. Spock, you must not—"

"The plague will not be brought to the surface. I am not here to threaten, but to seek help. In the event no antidote for the plague is found, the *Enterprise* will destroy itself before the next ship-day is over."

The Prefect had been absorbing all this stolidly. Now he suddenly looked suspicious as Spock continued.

"Commander Demos will be killed with the rest of us. I regret this. There is only one way to save him and to save the survivor we found on Dramia II, who can attest to the innocence of your prisoner. A great many lives and truths are at stake here, and only one man can find the solution to them all: Dr. McCoy. You must release him immediately. Temporarily, if you will—but no one else has the skill to find a possible antidote in the time that remains."

The Prefect considered for long seconds—understandable, in light of the barrage of information Spock had just thrown at him. His decision was obviously agonized, but firm.

"I cannot," he announced finally.

"The survivor, Kolti, is a witness for Dr. McCoy. He can testify for him. There are many others, of different races, on board the *Enterprise* who will die if he is not released. We may all die anyway, Dr. McCoy among us. If you have so little confidence in his medical ability, at least release him to die of the plague with his friends."

"You argue plausibly, Vulcan, but without facts."

"You must trust me. I have no other assurances to give."

The Prefect seemed to be a reasonable being. If Spock was interpreting the alien expression correctly, the Draymian leader was going through some tortuous mental gymnastics.

His expression turned crafty. "There is another who might persuade me. Let this witness, this claimed survivor, speak."

"Impossible. He, too, is seriously stricken."

Frustration all too suddenly replaced deliberation at the other end of the transmission. "Demos cannot speak, the witness cannot speak, even Captain Kirk cannot speak—yet you wish us to release the accused McCoy. On faith. Do you think you can secure the freedom of such a criminal so simply? Did you not think I would see through your desperate ploy?"

The screen went blank.

"McCoy," Kirk mumbled from behind Spock. "Got to get McCoy."

The first officer tried to re-establish the contact, but this time the ground station on Draymia refused to acknowledge his signals. He finally stopped trying, turned and walked over to Kirk.

"Captain, are you . . . ?"

"One minute I'm fine, the next I can taste oblivion—it's the stimulants, Mr. Spock. Uneven effect on the system, guesswork dosage . . . my body will pay for it in the end, I suppose. What about . . . ?"

Spock shook his head. "The Draymians refuse to release him. Unfortunately, they have no reason to trust us. They have a right to be cautious, but at the same time they are not reacting logically in this."

"No, Spock," Kirk breathed heavily, "they're reacting emotionally. I'm sorry so much of the universe turns out to be more unreasonable than Vulcan."

"It *is* distressing at times," Spock admitted, missing Kirk's sarcasm entirely. "But if you'll grant me the freedom to improvise in the face of adversity, I believe I can secure Dr. McCoy's release anyway."

Kirk stared painfully up at him. "That would mean contravening the official warrant, Mr. Spock."

"Only the letter, Captain. Dr. McCoy could be returned to stand trial afterward. I hardly need point out this is a desperation measure I am proposing. We will borrow Dr. McCoy for a little while. If we die, I do not think he will care what the Draymians do to him anyway."

"You're sure you can pull this off, Spock?"

"I intend to—"

"No, don't tell me." Kirk didn't have to think. He put his palms on the arm of the chair and shoved. Spock hurried to get a supportive arm under one shoulder.

"I think I can handle the transporter for you, Spock . . ."

"Be careful, Captain," the first officer admonished. They had staggered down to the transporter room. Spock waited within the alcove while Kirk adjusted the settings. "I would dislike materializing several kilometers above the streets of the capital city."

Kirk nodded, managed a grin, and engaged the instrumentation. There was something on his fevered mind, something else he had to ask Spock . . .

He hadn't thought of it by the time the first officer was gone.

It was dark where Spock rematerialized on the street parallel to the justice building. Dark and late.

He still felt exposed, but fortunately there appeared to be no strolling Draymians about to observe his arrival. Not that the average Draymian would pay much attention to him.

Unless, he mused distastefully, the Draymians had

better control of their emotions than their leaders had displayed thus far, the word of McCoy's arrest must have been kept secret. Otherwise a mob surely would have overrun the building by now. Hence he could expect to be regarded by the average citizen with curiosity rather than animosity.

This time he would turn the government's secrecy to his own advantage.

There were definite benefits in being smaller than the local inhabitants. It enabled Spock to make his way skillfully through the labyrinth of corridors in the building, dodging the night staff. The latter were too engrossed in their own drudgery to peer hard at places where Draymians would not fit.

But the two guards standing watch outside the chamber housing McCoy's force-cell were a different lot. They appeared fit, alert, and fully capable of rapid employment of the primitive but lethal-looking apparatus strapped at their waists.

For a moment Spock hesitated uncertainly, wondering at the presence of only two guards for so great a suspected criminal as McCoy. Then he realized that the doctor had been handed over freely. The Draymians had no reason to suppose the *Enterprise* would relinquish him only to take him back suddenly.

Hence the reason for Spock's haste—for if the Prefect had a little time to reflect on his recent conversation with him. . . .

Of one thing he was sure—this was not the time to debate the ethics of the situation with McCoy's guards. Such individuals were rarely selected for their receptiveness to logical persuasion or, for that matter, to original thought. He did not think they would react politely if he announced his intentions.

He slid a stylus from his waist, tossed it across the corridor. It clattered loudly in the quiet. Both guards were immediately alert. Hands on side-arms, they moved to investigate the source of the noise.

An unexpected bonus—Spock hadn't expected both of them leave their station. The unbarred portal to McCoy lay open.

But the guards hadn't looked incompetent. There-

fore, they weren't. Therefore, there was something unseen here to be wary of. Slipping noiselessly across the
hallway and into the chamber beyond, he quickly
discovered what. A quick block knocked the hand
weapon from the third guard waiting at the far wall.
But a pillarlike arm closed around Spock's waist, lifting
him high, squeezing, impairing his breathing.

With no time to experiment on an intractable subject, Spock reached around and back as massive arm
muscles tightened. Finding the spot he wanted, he
moved his fingers a certain way . . .

The guard collapsed with satisfying speed. When he
crumpled to the parquet floor, the sound was loud
enough to awaken the drowsing McCoy.

He rolled over on his bunk and stared. As soon as
he recognized Spock he was on his feet and over by the
inner wall of the cell.

"Spock—what in the world—"

Spock ignored the questions as he glanced back at
the open doorway. Apparently the two guards outside
were still searching for the source of the clattering. The
little control box slid clear of the guard's hip. Spock
studied it, touched the remembered sequence of
switches.

"Input later, Doctor—no time now. And keep your
voice down."

The first glowing nimbus that enclosed McCoy vanished. Another touch and the innner force-field disappeared. McCoy was trying to talk and awaken at the
same time. The resulting combination of questions and
accusations was understandably garbled.

"Have you and Jim gone out of your minds,
Spock?" he finished confusedly. "Why—this is a jail
break."

"If you'll just step out of the force-field area and
come with me, Doctor . . ."

McCoy took a step—backward. "Spock, I can't. It's
illegal. You saw the warrant. I've got to stand trial. I
want to stand trial." His face was agonized. "I have to
find out if—"

"You will stand trial and you will find out, Doctor,"
Spock insisted, impatiently looking from the recalci-

trant physician to the still vacant doorway. "After you've found an antidote for the plague which is about to kill everyone aboard the *Enterprise*."

McCoy started. "Plague . . . ?"

"We found a survivor, too, on Dramia II. A potential witness in your behalf. I do not know whether the disease lay dormant in him until he came aboard, or what. That is what you must discover. Humans are as susceptible to the disease as Draymians. Nearly everyone aboard is seriously ill."

"Spock—you don't tell me the important things first."

"You never ask me the important things first, Doctor."

McCoy moved quickly clear of the force-field boundary, outside the final bar to the ship's transporter beam.

"You realize, Doctor, the Draymians could still acquit you. But if you return aboard, you will be exposed to the disease. You could die, too."

Fully awake now, McCoy brushed hair from his eyes and glanced at him. "I'm aware of that—who's the doctor here? What surprises me is that you'd even think of mentioning it."

"I apologize, Doctor, but," Spock stared at the door, "I have been operating under stress lately." Out came the communicator. "We are clear of the force cell, Captain, beam us aboard."

A startled, angry voice sounded. Not from the communicator but from the doorway. The other two guards had returned. It took barely a second for them to take in the new alien, the fact that the prisoner stood alongside him instead of behind a glowing shield, and their unconscious companion of the floor.

A pair of tiny, explosive shells passed right through the place where McCoy and Spock had stood second-fractions before. They made a mess of the far wall.

IV

McCoy was mentally reviewing everything they knew about the Dramia II plague even as reintegration was being completed in the transporter alcove aboard ship. Scientific speculation vanished as soon as he saw Kirk, his skin now turned a bilious green, slumped over the transporter console.

"Jim!"

Kirk looked up, grinned weakly. "Hello, Bones. Welcome back." He collapsed before McCoy could set foot outside the alcove.

Kneeling next to Kirk, McCoy rolled him over and studied the weakened form as if the cause of the plague might suddenly advertise itself visibly—a movement under the skin, or glowing germs spelling out the formula for an effective serum.

Kirk only lay there.

"Help me get him to Sick Bay, Spock."

Together they wrestled the captain down to McCoy's lab, placed him alongside the other two who had first been stricken—Kolti and Demos.

The two Draymians and one human lay with a ghastly motionlessness. This was a quiet, efficient disease. There were no flailing arms, no hysterical gasps for air, no hallucinations and no screams of pain—Only the peculiarly horrible pigmentation change . . . to be followed by death.

Occasionally Kirk, still under the waning influence of the stimulant overdose, would awaken and mutter something half-coherent. McCoy didn't waste time listening to him.

Instead, he studied his friend as dispassionately as possible. Only by removing himself to a peak of empirical distraction would his mind stay clear enough to hunt for a solution.

He was aware that he had already been massively exposed to infection. Right up until the onset of the disease he should feel fine. First his ability to work and then his life would go in rapid succession.

It shouldn't be so hard. He should have been able to find a solution. But he hadn't. Couldn't.

McCoy pounded on the console of the medical computer as if it were personally responsible for the steadily approaching disaster. Every time he seemed to be coming close, the white letters, the same damning white letters, would suddenly flash on the annex screen . . .

NO CROSS-CORRELATION—PROPOSAL INEFFECTIVE

. . . and he'd have to start all over again. Doctor? Who said he was a doctor? He had fooled everyone long enough.

Bitterly, he mused that if the Draymians had been right all along, he was going to be executed by the plague he'd initiated. Not that he minded being subjected to such impersonal justice.

But he minded very much that all his friends might be taken along with him—victims of a more mature incompetence.

He looked over to where Spock was sitting. Calm, seemingly relaxed, the first officer studied another annex linked to the medical computer. They wouldn't find an antidote in there—of that McCoy had grown certain. But it probably helped relieve Spock's feeling of helplessness.

Besides, there was always the miniscule chance there might be *something* in the records that could lead to a hint of the relative of a clue.

Give him one straw . . .

"Anything at all, Spock?"

"Negative, Doctor."

McCoy studied his own readout, rubbed at his forehead. "The problem is that these violent pigmentation shifts don't link up with any known, or even with any rumored disease."

Doesn't link up, doesn't add up, no correlation, no correlation—but the pigmentation changes were the major symptom, weren't they? Well, weren't they?

Idly, he voiced a peripheral thought. "Spock, we know Vulcans are immune to this plague. That doesn't mean they couldn't be carriers."

"No, Doctor. It does not."

"Yet you still beamed down after me."

Spock didn't look up from his annex screen. "Given the Draymian's intransigence where your release was concerned, I felt justified in taking a calculated risk."

McCoy, then, was not the only one in this room whose conscience had reason to burn.

Something basic was wrong with their approach. Surely the Draymians had already exhausted this line of research. A first-year medical student, now, with a mind unencumbered by years of precedent, might have seen a solution instantly. But he, with a lifetime of statistics and experience crammed into his cranium, could not see through the muck of acquired knowledge. Was he even capable of having an original idea anymore?

Where was the freshness of youth when it was so desperately required?

He looked again at Demos, Kolti, Kirk. Their color had shifted to pink. Soon it would be bright red and then it wouldn't matter what brilliant insights, what revelations he would be privileged to glimpse.

"Work harder, Spock. They're entering the terminal stage."

"A useless admonition, Doctor."

It was. Spock was already driving himself as hard as he could. If he displayed no sign of it, it was because not an iota of energy was wasted in visible muscle tension or in nervous breathing.

McCoy even tried a tight-beam transmission in hopes of contacting Alco III, the nearest Federation world with advanced medical facilities. That failed him, too.

"Spock ... Spock!" he yelled, trying to break the first officer from his transfixed study of the computer annex. "I'm trying to get through to Alco. Maybe it's too far, but . . .," he squinted at the viewscreen, "I shouldn't be getting the kind of scrambled readings I am."

Spock looked over at him, spoke with doleful assurance. "That is hardly surprising, Doctor. Undoubtedly one of the numerous auroral disturbances is now placed between Draymia and Alco. Even a tight beam could not penetrate such a vast disturbance."

He was on his own. He had lost precious minutes hoping for the aid of a distant angel. McCoy finally shut off the annex and simply sat back, to think. Behind him, Kirk was mumbling. He had overheard their last conversation and even his subconscious was attuned to the beauties of the universe he loved so well.

"Local phenomenon ... auroral excitation, lovely, lovely ... change colors, shift hues, magnificent ...

"*Aesculapius!*" McCoy yelled.

"No need to shout, Doctor," Spock said imperturbably. "You have found something?"

"The auroras ..."

"Are a dead-end, Doctor. They are of a peculiar nature, but radiation levels are far from lethal—far from being even slightly dangerous."

McCoy rose from his seat and stretched. "One day, Spock, I'll sit down and correlate the relationship of the auroral radiation to its effect on the melanin in human—and Draymian—skin. But not now."

Spock looked thoughtful for a long minute, then became almost excited. "The pigmentation changes are *not* a symptom of the disease. They are a separate effect caused by the auroral radiation."

McCoy nodded vigorously. "Feed the same data we've been using into the med computer, *without* making any mention of epidermal tone shift. See if we get a result this time."

Spock didn't hesitate. Changing the input program required only a minute. There was a brief pause . . . and then words and figures started pouring back at them.

"Fast," was all McCoy said.

"I believe this is what you need, Doctor," Spock observed, studying the steadily maturing formula.

McCoy sat down, realized he was shaking slightly. "The color change in the skin had nothing whatsoever to do with the plague. We reported them as a symptom ... no wonder the computer couldn't correlate it with the rest of our information.

"It's giving us an antidote ... and as to the cause of the disease," he sighed, "it's the aurora, too."

"But, Doctor," Spock began uncertainly, "you just said it was a separate effect."

"It is, but the radiation is also the key to the plague. It just doesn't have any link with the color changes. There must be a virus, a bacterium, which is stimulated by the auroral radiation. Naturally, since the aurora is stimulating both, it would appear the color shift is a result of the disease—when in fact, they have no medical connection." He paused.

"Nineteen years ago Dramia II must have been passing through another of the strong auroral belts. I can't be sure ... I wasn't in astronomy. But I'll bet a check of the expedition's records will confirm it. I do seem to remember a colorful night sky, though. I was too busy to admire local color most of the time." His voice dropped.

"Death's rainbow—it brought on the original plague, just as this aurora has brought it on again. We weren't affected until a carrier of the dormant microbe— Kolti—was brought aboard. I think a check of old records on Draymia itself might show legends of people changing color ... and returning to normal when the auroras passed on."

His voice dropped to a whisper. Spock didn't press for clarification—the relief that had appeared in McCoy's voice was a private thing, not to be interrupted or shared. It was a relief that could not be judged on any general human scale ... only on the personal one of Dr. Leonard McCoy.

"I had nothing to do with the plague, then." He blinked and walked over to stand behind Spock, peering over his shoulder at the screen.

"There's our virus, just as you suspected, Doctor." Spock worked the instrumentation and a new flow of information appeared. "And there is the declaration I most feared."

Under the microphoto of the virus itself had appeared the words, "NO KNOWN ANTIDOTE."

Spock tried to keep his voice as comforting as possible. "I suspected that if there were a cure, the Draymians would have found it. With nineteen years in which to research, even theoretically, they must have hit upon the same aurora-plague connection we've just reached."

"Every disease caused by a living agent has an antidote, Spock. Every . . ." He stopped, his voice sharpening. *"Think, Spock."*

"I have been, Doctor. It took me a moment to make the . . . correlation. Do you remember our witness . . . Kolti? You treated him nineteen years ago for saurian virus."

"The individual . . . there were so many. Maybe . . . yes, I think I do. It was a strange case to find on Dramia II. As I recall, he was one of their off-world representatives. Contracted it from someone in the Federation. Sure, I remember him now! We had a helluva time digging out the right serum for that . . . we'd expected to have to treat only local infections. Wait a minute." McCoy's face lit up like one of engineer Scott's control reactors.

"You say *he's* the witness, the survivor you found?"

"Correct, Doctor. He survived the plague and all aftereffects. Apparently, however, inoculation against saurian virus does not last nineteen years."

"No. No, it doesn't. He needs a booster. In fact, everyone on board ought to have a similar injection. If the key *is* saurian antibodies, recovery from the plague after administration should be as rapid as debilitation was."

"Let us hope so, Doctor," Spock remarked with a glance at the nearby beds. Kolti, Kirk and Demos were beginning to turn a dark crimson. "We have very little time."

McCoy was already moving toward the refrigerated locker where preprepared serums were stored.

"I'd like to run some tests on this first, Spock, but as you say, we haven't time." He grimaced. "Any side effects can't be worse than death."

"A queerly logical statement, Doctor." Spock understood the principles of irony.

McCoy hurriedly filled a mass injector, then a second, with three-quarters of the available serum. Then he programmed the organic fabrication computer to prepare the necessary remainder. It would be ready long before he and Spock had finished applying the first doses.

The infirmary was soon filled with hisses from the hypo sprays as they moved from bed to bed, pallet to cot, administering the antidote. Nor had McCoy neglected himself—if for some reason the serum proved ineffective, he wanted to be the first to know.

There was a buzz from the intercom set next to the computer keyboard. McCoy looked up uncertainly. "I thought you said everyone else aboard was incapacitated, Spock."

"They are, Doctor," he replied, heading for the *acknowledge* switch, "but the main computer itself is also immune to the plague."

McCoy muttered something about "Vulcans and machines" which Spock didn't hear and continued inoculating the prone crew members scattered through the room. Spock returned a moment later.

"You will be interested to know, Doctor, that we are leaving the last streamer of the aurora which caused this trouble and blocked your communications attempt. Also, I ran a check on the composition of Draymian and Dramian atmospheres. I don't think we'll unearth any historical records of mass color changes on Draymia. The composition differs slightly but significantly ... enough to block out the melanin-affecting radiation of the auroras."

McCoy moved to the next body. "So Draymia's always been plague-immune. No wonder the outburst on Dramia II terrified them so. They'd no experience with even the color shifts."

He made the inoculation, noticed that the indicator light on the side of the sprayer had come on.

"Empty ... the synthesizer should be finished with the big batch I ordered up. Be right back, Spock." The first officer nodded, continued work with his own spray as McCoy started back toward the far end of the infirmary and the medical lab.

On the way he saw that Kirk, Demos and Kolti were running the color change backward. Red, to pink, then green and blue and finally their normal healthy color again. The speed of the change was fast enough to be visible to the naked eye—hopefully physical recovery would be equally rapid.

It was. When McCoy returned with a second empty hypo, Kirk had already opened his eyes. Seconds later Kolti and Demos followed suit. Nearby, a transporter specialist was snuffling like a pig in clover as he, too, started to come around.

Kirk looked at the ceiling, then rolled his head sideways. He looked tired, but had already regained enough strength to smile and nod at McCoy.

A strange disease—he would spend considerable time analyzing it. Studying with rather more detachment than he had been permitted up to now.

It would make a paper suitable for submission to the *Starfleet Medical Journal*—was that a tear at the corner of one eye? He wiped it away before any of his patients could notice—too much close work in too brief a time, that was all.

"You did it, Bones," Kirk mumbled softly.

"Again." McCoy looked up, past the stirring form of Kirk, to see a tall Draymian he didn't recognize staring back at him. The alien wore a look which even a child could have read as undisguised admiration.

He turned away, embarrassed by both the unabashed adulation and the fact that for the life of him he couldn't place the face of this survivor. But then, there had been so many Draymians those long days years ago. But undoubtedly this Kolti had seen very few humans, so it was natural that he should remember the doctor.

Nevertheless, he walked over to the stranger and ex-

changed hand clasps and Draymian embrace with him.
The patient's crushing affection was an excellent sign
his body was rapidly returning to normal.

Kirk was sitting up on the edge of his bed, exercising
his neck with circling twists of his head.

"How do you feel, Jim?"

"Like I've been asleep for ten thousand years,
Bones, and in all that time no one bothered to dust
me."

"Dr. McCoy?" He turned and saw that the Commander of Draymian security was also sitting up, a
mite awkwardly, on his undersized bed. "We are a
technologically advanced race, Dr. McCoy. We had
thought that in a few things, such as interstellar travel
and contact, we are still in our infancy. It seems that
we are still in our infancy in less scientific ways as
well."

He extended a huge hand. "Will you accept the sin-
cere apologies of a misguided child who knew no better
and had only his civilization's best interests at heart?
The malice lies in our memory of events, not in our
hearts."

McCoy shook the proffered hand firmly, then moved
on—he still had work to do.

"Doctor," Spock called, from where he was administering the serum, "are you certain that *you* are all
right?"

McCoy wiped moisture from his eyes. "Doesn't anyone understand basic physiology around here!" he
snarled. "I'm working hard and under stress, that's
all."

Spock linked the phrase with the tone of McCoy's
voice and his hypothetical mental state—and understood. Of course, he saw no reason to smile.

If the Draymians had been careful at first to conceal
their enmity, they showed unbridled enthusiasm when
making amends. There were times during the following
days when McCoy thought he would have to run and
hide lest he be smothered by constant accolades. The
Draymian people outdid themselves in their gratitude.

The only difficulties arose when he was forced time

and again to refuse actual gifts, explaining that regulations forbade accepting any kind of gratuity, however indirect, for services rendered in the line of duty. Their good health, he told them, was reward enough.

When the last medal had been awarded, the last speech read, the final hyperbolic hyperbole driven home, they found themselves outside the justice building once again, high above the bustling streets and boulevards of the capital of Draymia.

Kirk and Spock were there with McCoy, all three resplendent in full dress uniform. The Prefect was there, and Demos, of course. And a third Draymian—Kolti, now toweringly splendid in the blue and puce of Draymian Deep Space Service, Diplomatic Section.

They were going to see a lot more of that well-cut uniform in the future, Kirk surmised quietly—especially if Kolti was an indication of the kind of people being trained to fill it.

" .. and so we of Draymia wish to thank you once more, Dr. McCoy," the Prefect was concluding, "for the discovery of the antidote which frees future colonies from destruction by the auroral plague."

"Thank Mr. Spock and Captain Kirk, not me," McCoy told him. He managed not to blush—he had already blushed himself out, these past few days. At least, he thought he had, until the Prefect suddenly produced an intimidating scroll from out of nowhere.

"And now," the alien official began, "it is my pleasure to relate some fitting personal sentiments on commemoration of—"

"Please, your Prefectship," McCoy broke in tiredly. "Somehow I have the feeling I've heard these sentiments before. Couldn't I—please—beg off? I'd really like to get back to the ship."

"We must apologize," Demos said, coming to McCoy's rescue by placing a restraining yet gentle hand on the disappointed Prefect's arm. There was no telling how long the security chief had worked on his *own* as yet concealed speech. "But as great a genius as Dr. McCoy is," he continued, "he has not yet discovered an antidote for boredom."

Kirk and the Prefect laughed, while Spock looked normally phlegmatic.

"I'm afraid," McCoy sallied in reply, "that while that's a disease rampant throughout the Galaxy, it's barely been touched upon."

The Prefect made the Draymian equivalent of a resigned sigh and folded up his lengthy scroll. "Very well, then . . . go in peace and health, Dr. McCoy—the health you have given to future settlers. We will see you again some day, I hope."

"I have a hunch Federation vessels will be calling at Draymia with increasing frequency, sir," Kirk predicted. "I wouldn't be surprised if we were assigned another stop here. We'll be looking forward to it."

"It is well, then," the Prefect concluded, satisfied.

Embraces were exchanged all around. Then the three officers stepped back toward the ornamental railing.

"Beam us aboard, Mr. Scott."

"Aye, Captain," came the chief engineer's happy acknowledgment back over the communicator.

"I don't know about you, gentlemen," Kirk said as the elevator carried them toward the Bridge, "but I'm ready to get back to Alco Starbase."

"And I," McCoy informed them fervently, "am about ready to get back to the normal, daily routine of passing out pink pills and examining sore throats!"

"I would hope such exotic efforts," Spock began as the doors slid apart and they entered the Bridge, "would include resumption of the normal, daily dispensing of the regular vitamin rations to the crew, in proper proportions according to their biological requirements."

McCoy hesitated just inside the portal. "What's that supposed to mean?"

"Well, you *have* been somewhat derelict in your duties of late, Doctor."

McCoy gaped at him. "Derelict in my duties? I've been held in solitary confinement on an alien world, accused of mass murder, and forced to find an antidote for a previously incurable plague in an incredibly short

period of time—with only your help, I might add—and
you can say I've been derelict in my duties?"

"Hippocrates," Spock replied calmly, "would not
have approved of attempts at finding lame excuses,
Doctor." He called the elevator and stepped inside,
leaving Kirk and a flabbergasted McCoy alone by the
doorway.

McCoy proceeded to make several unidentifiable
mouth noises, none with complimentary overtones,
which seemed to relate vaguely to Spock's ancestry.

"Calm down, Bones," Kirk finally told him, working
hard to stifle a smile. "You know Spock—he's just trying to get your goat."

"Goat," McCoy sputtered, "I'll give him my goat . . .
with anthrax, yet!" There was a wild look coming into
his eyes. "Jim, do you think Vulcans are subject to
anthrax? Do you think they're vulnerable to—"

Kirk couldn't contain himself any longer. He broke
out laughing, was joined by Uhura, Sulu, and the high,
amused piping of Arex. McCoy glanced around the
room, immediately saw he would get no sympathy from
this bunch.

He finally got hold of his emotions. "Jim, if I'm ever
in jail again, don't send a Vulcan to release me. If you
do, you'll have to send someone else to drag him out.
You'll have to!"

He became silent then, and the wild look was replaced with a smile of uncommonly fiendish glee. It so-
bered Kirk.

"Bones," he asked worriedly, "what are you conjur-
ing?"

"Vitamin supplements," McCoy was muttering. He
sounded almost cheerful, "Yes, vitamin supplements."
He looked up. "Excuse me, everybody . . . I have some
work to do . . . some supplements to prepare. I've been
derelict in my daily duties."

Kirk could hear him singing something about vitamin supplements until the turbolift carried him out of
range.

PART II

THE PRACTICAL JOKER

(Adapted from a script by Chuck Menville)

V

"Since I have evidentally failed to make myself clear so far, Nurse Chapel, I will repeat it once more," Spock told her tautly. "Vulcans are *not* subject to dandruff."

Chapel leaned back in the office chair and eyed the first officer of the *Enterprise* compassionately.

"Perhaps there is a different Vulcan term for it, then."

"Such a disease is *not* possible," Spock insisted. He scratched behind one ear. "However, I am compelled to admit that for an impossible affliction, it is proving most distracting."

"What is?" Both turned as McCoy walked in. "Hello, Christine. Hello, Spock. Is something the matter?" His voice was overflowing with innocence.

"Something has been the matter for a number of days, Doctor. Ever since we departed Draymia and before we began the survey of this non-system grouping of type-four asteroids." He glanced back across the desk.

"Nurse Chapel insists I have contracted a disease common only to decadent physiological systems, something she identifies as *dandruff*. I have explained patiently that Vulcans are not subject to such primitive afflictions."

"Yes, it's an affliction common to the inefficient human organism ... and it seems," McCoy added, leaning over to stare pointedly at Spock's scalp, "that you have an advanced case of it. My, my ... no wonder you've seemed so peevish lately."

"I am never peevish, and I tell you," Spock said in exasperation, "I do not have it. It is simply not possible for—you are smiling, Doctor. I don't believe anything I've said can be taken as amusing."

"Been getting your daily vitamin supplements, Spock? I know I was badly neglectful . . . you reminded me though. Remember?"

"Yes, I have to admit that you have returned to schedule with admira—" The first officer suddenly paused. If it was possible for a Vulcan to take on a suspicious expression, Spock had just acquired one.

"Vitamins . . . Doctor, is it possible that you harbored some irrational resentment against me for the comments I made regarding your efficiency, on our departure from Draymia? Is it possible that you . . . ?"

Spock rose abruptly from the chair. "I do not think," he said coldly, "that an analysis of my supplements will be necessary."

McCoy allowed himself a smile. "Oh, don't be so stiff about it, Spock. Besides, it can only worsen your condition. I'll remove the additive I put into your supplements immediately, and your primitive affliction will vanish in a couple of days. In exchange, we won't hear anything more about my performance as ship's doctor for a while . . . will we?"

"Is that a request," Spock asked, still frozen, "or a threat?"

"Let's call it a reasonable adjustment of circumstances, arrived at by mutual consent of two intelligent beings. I could have arranged for something rather more radical than dandruff, you know. Besides, I'd think you'd find the situation interesting, from a scientific point of view. I didn't even know if it would work. Always nice to see theory confirmed. As far as I know, you're the first Vulcan in history to be plagued with—"

"Please, Doctor. I agree. Just correct it, please."

"All right, Spock, relax." The grin again. "It's not fatal." He walked past the desk and punched out commands on the computer annex there.

"Something you might be interested in—here's the molecular schematic I had to design to produce the proper results. Took a neat little bit of organic doodling, I can tell you. Vulcans have so many antibodies in their blood it's almost impossible to find something to penetrate all those generations of acquired defenses."

"I'm sure, Doctor," Spock said dryly, peering at the diagram of bonded atoms on the screen, "that it taxed your abilities considerably."

"Speaking of taxing our skills," Nurse Chapel wondered aloud, "how much longer are we going to be stuck on this mineralogical survey before we can continue on back to Alco Starbase for a little rest and recreation?"

Glad of a chance to change the subject, Spock explained. "The extent and density of this free cluster has exceeded all previous drone estimates. Despite this, the captain estimates that we are now several days ahead of schedule. He is as anxious as the rest of us to be done with what is really a minor operation and he sorely resented the orders when they came through.

"Orders remain orders, however. We should be finished with the survey any day. A great deal of value has been learned, even if the learning has been monotonous. The cluster appears to offer considerable commercial promise. The asteroid masses are all irregular in shape, probably the remains of an exploded planet which tore loose from its parent system. Nonetheless they have remained tightly packed together. Some are of considerable size and a few are much larger than Ceres in the Sol system. I venture to say that within a few years the activity here will—"

There was a deep rumble and everything shook.

Chapel nearly fell backward out of the chair. Both Spock and McCoy had to grab for the computer console to steady themselves. The tremor died away quickly, leaving them suddenly tense. McCoy and Chapel exchanged nervous glances.

An alarm began to sound. From time to time short rumbles rose above the wail and irregular vibrations could be felt underfoot. But the first, serious jolt was not repeated.

"You okay, Christine?"

"Fine, but what happened?"

"I don't know." He looked over at Spock. "What do you think? Spock? Where'd he disappear to?"

Spock was already on his way to the Bridge. Only a very few things could produce the shaking and accompanying rumble they had experienced. Most of them were natural. Only one was artificial in origin. Experience told him it was the latter. They were under fire.

He emerged on the Bridge in time to see the main viewscreen overloaded by a blinding white glare. It faded slowly, the imagery reforming as the ship's scanners strove to recover from the intense dose of light.

He acknowledged a perfunctory greeting from Scott, who stood at the Bridge Engineering Station, as he made his way to the library-computer console.

The familiar whooping cry of the red-alert alarm was louder here on the Bridge, in deference to any sufferers in Sick Bay. He knew it was sounding the length and breadth of the battle cruiser.

Another blast rattled the Bridge enough to separate feet from deck momentarily, despite the artificial gravity. Yet another blast in the same place from a slightly more powerful photon bomb, and Spock's feet would leave the deck permanently.

Behind him Kirk's voice resounded—terse, businesslike—in complete control, although the source of the mysterious attack was still unknown.

"Scotty, give us maximum shielding, full power on the deflectors."

"Aye, Captain." Scott carried out the order, then turned his post over to a panting, just-arrived subordinate. The chief's place was back in Engineering Control, and he headed there in haste.

"Photon bombs," Uhura muttered. "But who?"

Kirk ignored the lieutenant's musing. "Mr. Sulu, bring us about to a new heading. One hundred twenty degrees north, up twenty. Initiate evasive pattern one."

"Aye sir," the helmsman responded promptly, working the instruments.

Kirk's businesslike manner now found a moment for open anger. "Mr. Spock, where were you?"

"I have no real excuse, Captain. I was suffering from

a prolonged distortion of subcutaneous follicular tissue."

"Yes, I noticed it. But if you don't find out who's attacking us, you're liable to have it cured forever."

"My own opinion exactly, Captain."

The requisite information was already appearing on the sensor screens above his station. To complement the printed readouts, the computer provided him with a three-dimensional schematic of their pursuers, along with classification, type, armament, displacement, number of crew and probable port of origin.

At the moment all the statistics were superfluous. "Romulans, Captain." He studied the main viewscreen, which still showed their last survey target—an enormous, rapidly shrinking hunk of stellar debris the size of a small moon.

"Apparently they were lying in wait for us on the far side of that major asteroid."

"By the Thane of Comorron!" came a furious voice. The burr was unmistakable. Scott had reached Engineering and when he'd overheard Spock's pronouncement, had yelled through the line Kirk had left open. "A cold-blooded ambush! That's goin' a bit far, even furr the Romulans. Let's give the cowards a fight they won't fergit!"

Kirk sympathized with his chief engineer, but kept his tone even as he hit the broadcast return. "Negative, Mr. Scott. I've already received several damage reports. Combined with the fact that we appear to be outnumbered three to one, I think we'd better settle for some well-directed name-calling."

"Discretion is the better part of valor, sir? I've always felt that was a bit of a contradiction in terms."

"Just stand by to give me all the power you can spare from the deflectors, Mr. Scott."

"Aye, sir," Scott said, making no effort to hide the disappointment in his voice. Kirk switched Engineering off. Sometimes Scott's spirit ran away with his better sense.

"Sulu, give me full power on the rear sensors."

"Aye, Captain."

The view in the main screen shifted as more explosions flared around the ship. Now though, under battle conditions, the visual scanners were automatically compensating for the intense radiation.

The three ships were tiny flecks, but Kirk felt he could make out the distinctive outlines, coming straight for them.

"The Romulans continue to pursue, Captain," Spock reported. "And they are increasing their speed. They also appear to be separating further, changing from attack position to an intricate entrapment maneuver."

"Can we outrun them, Mr. Spock?"

Spock hesitated, studying readouts as fast as the battle computer could supply them. "Indeterminate, Captain. With three ships in pursuit, prediction becomes extremely complex."

"Keep working on it." Lips set tight together, Kirk turned his attention back to the viewscreen and muttered under his breath. "They must want us badly to continue to pursue after their initial attack failed. Too late now for them to plead accident." His expression twisted into a faint grin. "The Romulans are coming." His voice rose as he called to Spock.

"Uncertainty's a hereditary factor with them. I think somebody got nervous and jumped the gun on us. If they'd waited till we were just a few kilometers closer to that big rock, we wouldn't have had a chance."

"True, Captain," Spock conceded. "They must have been observing our progress through the cluster for some time. Fortunately, our survey pattern varied according to the size and density of the asteroids themselves. They could not be entirely certain when we would alter course, hence someone's mounting fear we might suddenly discover their presence.

"Captain?" Kirk turned to look back at Uhura. "I've received an incoming transmission from the commander of the Romulan force. We have visual, too." She grinned. "He seems anxious to talk to you."

"I'll bet," Kirk replied grimly. "Put him through ... I've got a couple of things to say to him."

The sinister view of the three pursuing cruisers was replaced with a momentary flash of static, and then the sharp portrait of a smug Romulan officer.

Kirk disliked him on sight, even more than he did the usual example of Romulan militarism. He wasted no time on diplomatic niceties.

"Whoever you are, I demand an immediate explanation for this unprovoked attack."

"Unprovoked!" the Romulan echoed with mock anxiety. "My dear Captain Kirk, your ship trespassed into Romulan territory in defiance of our treaty. We had no choice but to defend ourselves and the sovereignty of the Empire."

"I know," Kirk shot back, "our appearance was a complete surprise to you."

"A terrible shock," the Romulan admitted.

"Which is how you happen to know my name."

"We, uh .. ," the Romulan coughed delicately, "recognized the serial number of your ship, and it is widely known who commands the Federation's famed *Enterprise.*"

"I see. Then perhaps you can explain this odd discrepancy?"

The alien commander was put off stride. "Discrepancy?"

"Yes. If your detectors have improved to the point that you can pick out our serial numbers at this distance, how come they failed to tell you that we're nowhere near Romulan territory? We were surveying an unclaimed asteroid cluster lying on the Federation border—well outside the farthest Romulan claim.

"I deny your blatantly artifical charge and plan to file a detailed complaint with the Romulan delegate to the Federation."

The commander was not upset. He even managed a smile, of a sort. "This ignores reality, Captain. You forget that invasion of Imperial territory is punishable by death. You and your crew have already been tried and convicted."

"I told you," Kirk said angrily, "we've committed no violation of Romulan boundaries. We're not subject to your legal farce."

"Details, details," came the unperturbed reply. "Oh, I suppose some blithering clerk might find a flaw in our reasoning ... but you will unfortunately not have an opportunity to file that complaint with him." He became positively charming.

"It is a pity you fail to recognize the inevitability of your situation, Captain. Why not surrender your vessel? We might arrange some kind of accommodation—leniency for some of your common ratings, say."

Kirk's stomach turned over. "Why don't you arrange . . . ?" he began heatedly. But the screen abruptly went dark. Perhaps something in Kirk's tone hinted to the Romulan commander that he wasn't going to agree to terms.

Another strong concussion rocked the Bridge.

"Captain," Spock reported, "the Romulan attack may have been hasty, but their closing formation is well conceived. I can find no evasive pattern that will enable us to escape from more than two ships at a time. Regardless of how we maneuver, there will always be one cruiser within range.

"If we turn to fight it, and fail to dispatch it immediately, we will soon be forced to exchange fire with all three. Our deflectors will be unable to handle such a concentration of firepower. Conversely, if we continue to run, it appears that all three will close on us eventually, producing the same untenable position."

Kirk thought furiously. "I disagree about our ability to handle all three of them in a last-ditch fight, Mr. Spock. But I wouldn't put it past one of the Romulan captains to exchange his ship and crew for clan glory by making a suicide charge at us while the others keep us occupied. Our deflectors could never handle that kind of overload."

Spock nodded. "The importance the Romulans attach to certain archaic forms of self-sacrifice is well known. I agree that from the standpoint of the Romulan High Command, the elimination of the *Enterprise* is of such importance that they wouldn't consider the sacrifice of a single cruiser excessive."

"Which means we've got to try and run—somehow," Kirk decided.

The conversation was interrupted by several strange beeps and whines from the navigation console and helm.

"What is it, Mr. Sulu?"

The helmsman was studying his instrumentation with a peculiar grimace of uncertainty. "Captain, we are approaching an unlisted energy field of considerable extent, and I'm getting some mighty odd readings from the sensor scans."

"Mr. Spock?"

"A moment, Captain." Once more the view of the Romulan cruiser dead astern disappeared as Spock engaged the forward scanners.

Ahead, emblazoned across the starfield, lay an enormous mass of light that looked like a lambent fog bank.

"Partially gaseous," Spock informed them, "but also heavily particulate. The difference is still undeterminable. It appears to be a mass of minute energized particles held together by a force other than gravity—it's far too dense to be, say, a nebular fragment. And Lieutenant Sulu is right—the readings are *most* peculiar.

"Odd that such a unique phenomenon is not on the charts made by the drone that surveyed the asteroidal cluster. Even a drone should have detected such a concentration of energy this close by."

"As far as I'm concerned it came out of a brass bottle," Kirk said excitedly. "It may be just what we need to shake the Romulans. You know how reluctant they are to have anything to do with anything radically unfamiliar. They're appropriators—not explorers."

Spock's reply held a mild warning tone: "Not always an unwise policy, Captain." He gestured toward the screen. "This field registers very strong, and it contains internal subatomic configurations of a still unidentifiable nature."

"We'll have plenty of time to puzzle them out, Mr. Spock, *after* we've shaken the Romulans. Lieutenant Uhura, general order. Secure for emergency running. Mr. Sulu, take us through."

"Yes, *sir!*" Sulu adjusted the helm, and the *Enterprise* changed course slightly, plunging straight into the outermost edge of the luminescent barrier.

"If I may say so, Captain," Spock commented, keeping his attention focused on the sensors that were now registering their passage through the strange field, "your decision was rather hasty. Influenced, I believe, by emotional considerations."

"You bet it was, Mr. Spock," Kirk admitted without rancor. "I weighed all the facts, considered all the evidence—including your own information concerning our probable inability to escape by running or defending against a concerted three-pronged attack. I admit the thought of being blown to bits prompted me to take a bit of a risk. If that's emotionalism—"

"We are entering the inner region of the field, Captain," the first officer observed, thus putting an end to the debate.

A steady vibration had sprung up underfoot. Kirk felt it first in his feet, then all over as it increased, working its way up his body. Despite the effect, his body wasn't vibrating, of course—merely feeling the effects of the oscillating ride as transmitted through the fabric of the ship.

A fantastic parade of abstract forms and images exploded toward them on the main screen as the *Enterprise* sailed through the sea of energy. Colors so brilliant, hues so intense they seemed to have a solid presence. Deep maroons and light yellows, forest greens, blues, blacks, electric pink—a whole region that passed by instantly and had the texture of blackberry milk, another that resembled rutilated quartz lit from within.

Kirk had little time to appreciate the beauty rushing at him. His concern now was with the destructive effects of all that riotous radiation. The vibrations intensified. His voice was jittery when he spoke, from the vibration, not from internal insecurity.

"What are our chances, Mr. Spock."

The first officer of the *Enterprise* was already attempting the near-impossible task of monitoring the readouts with one eye and gauging the composition of the surrounding field with the other, fighting to keep quarks and ergs on the proper sides of his scientific ledger.

"If the intensity and density—the interrelation is vital—does not increase beyond the subatomic, we should be able to continue safe passage. If it rises, our shields will be hard pressed to ward it off."

Kirk gave a curt nod, reached to activate the intercom. It vibrated like a chair massager under his fingertips.

"Mr. Scott, how are things at your end?"

"From the sound of your voice, Captain, no worse than they are on the Bridge. It's hard to tell whether the shields are workin' at all, at times. Strangest arrangement of energy I've seen in some time, and I'm gettin' readings from the dilithium reaction chambers you wouldn't believe. But ... everythin' appears to be runnin' all right."

"According to Mr. Spock, the field we're passing through is composed of very dense, unusually charged subatomic particles."

"Mad matter. That explains some of the readings I'm gettin', then—but not all of 'em, Captain. I don't mind tellin' you I'll be glad when we're clear of this."

"Glad to hear you're bothered, Scotty. If the readouts trouble *you*, they ought to give the Romulans the collywobbles. Kirk out."

"Scott out." He clicked off the intercom and placed one hand on the smooth arc of wall nearby as he studied the gauges which monitored the heartbeat of the *Enterprise*.

"Hold together, little darlin' ... hold together ..."

The energy field was larger than initial estimates indicated, but by interstellar standards it was still an insignificant stain in the endless vacuum.

An insignificant stain, Kirk reflected as he studied the thinning panoply of color, that might save all their lives.

"Maintain this heading, Mr. Sulu. Mr. Spock, we have readings taken from both sides of the mass now ... what's its configuration and how does it relate to our present situation?"

"According to the computer calculations, Captain, the field appears to be thick enough so that if the Romulans attempt to go around it, we will easily succeed in outdistancing them."

"I think they just reached that same conclusion,

Captain," Sulu reported. "I can still pick out their engines through all that concentrated small stuff, and it looks like they've turned back. At the very least, they've slowed to a crawl on the opposite side. Doesn't look like they're going to chance it."

"Stay on those scanners, Mr. Sulu," Kirk ordered. "They may try coming through slowly."

But when there was no sign of their pursuers seconds or even crucial minutes later, he felt safe in taking the ship off red alert.

"No sign of them, sir," Sulu breathed in relief. "It worked."

"They turned back rather than risk the field's unknown potential," Kirk agreed.

Spock turned philosophical. "The percentages would appear to be in the Romulans favor, Captain. From their standpoint the glory is greater if they destroy us in battle. However, if we perish through natural causes such as the energy field, their ultimate objective is still attained. Logically, there was no reason to risk themselves."

"All the same, Spock," he insisted, "they may remain nearby evaluating the field and eventually they may determine they can make the passage safely. They know we've suffered damage, which that rocky journey might have aggravated. We still may see them." He looked to the helm.

"We'll lay to here for repairs, Mr. Sulu. Inform the necessary sections to hurry their work, especially Engineering."

Uhura was rubbing the section of her anatomy that was most often in contact with the ship. "After that ride, I could use some repairs," she observed feelingly.

"I suppose," Kirk theorized, "that what's needed in such cases is an extremely localized deflector field."

"I would suggest," Spock added dryly, "the problem be proposed to Chief Scott. I am sure he would find the mechanics of the problem most stimulating."

"You'd better keep a close eye on the chief, though, Lieutenant. He's a devil with those calipers."

Uhura eyed them both with distaste. "I suppose you both think you're terribly amusing."

Spock looked querulous. "Amusing, Lieutenant Uhura? I can assure you I was merely trying to . . ."

The elevator doors dilated. "Reporting for duty, Captain," a high voice said.

"Good timing, Mr. Arex. You take over." Kirk rose from the chair. "I'd like to make a personal survey of the damaged sections and then take that overdue mid-meal."

Damage from the Romulan photon bombs proved erratic, but there was enough destruction to give somber evidence of what could have happened. Fortunately, Romulan discipline had a way of breaking down when a large measure of glory was at stake. If the captains of the three cruisers had been able to present a coordinated attack at the optimum moment, now . . .

They were lucky it hadn't been a Klingon attack. By now a Klingon commander would have executed the entire Fire-Control section for jumping the gun.

As it was, there was some severe damage in Engineering—though nothing irreparable. Not for the resourceful Scott and his people. Also, concussion from near-misses had battered several storage compartments, and nearly hulled the shuttlecraft hangar. Personal injury was minor, however, and there were no fatalities, since the damage had been wrought in unmanned areas. These were easily sealed off. Repair crews, under the direction of engineers Kaplan and Senif, were making rapid progress in repairing the battered sections.

In the upper Officer's Mess, Kirk had joined Spock, Uhura, McCoy and Sulu for what he had hoped would be a leisurely mid-meal. They might not have a chance to eat for some time if the Romulans decided to try a sudden move through the energy cloud.

Scott joined them soon after they began. The chief engineer had been supervising steadily and only now felt satisfied enough to take a break.

He took a long draught of the contents of the huge mug he carried with him. Irish coffee, Kirk noted. He doubted there was another engineer in the fleet who could program a standard naval galley to produce Irish coffee—or Russian, Jamaican, Turkish, Balaklavan, Austrian and the host of additional caffeinic concoctions Scott could brew on demand. The same brand of ingenuity had kept the *Enterprise* one step ahead of disaster on more occasions than he cared to recall.

"How are repairs coming, Scotty?" Kirk inquired, knowing full well Scott wouldn't be present if any serious difficulties remained. But the chief would feel slighted if he wasn't asked.

"Better than I hoped, when I first saw what the heathen's bombs had done." He took a barbecued rib from his tray and bit deep.

"Another couple of seconds in getting full power to the screens, though—as it is, we'll be good as new in another twenty hours." His expression turned sour. "No thanks to those Romulan vultures."

"The Romulans are not even distantly ornithoid, Mr. Scott. I am surprised that you . . ." Spock grew aware of the amused silence. "I see," he said thoughtfully, "another terran colloquial expression."

"I was referrin', Mr. Spock, to the Romulans' social habits, not their anatomy. Though I could make some suitable comments regardin' that." There were mutters of agreement from around the table.

They'd been very lucky, Kirk mused. He considered the framework of his official report. This was no case of mistaken identity, and there was no question of a misplaced boundary, despite the claim of the Romulan commander.

The ambush had been planned in advance and nearly brought off. Only the overeagerness of some fire-control officer and the presence of the drifting energy field had saved them.

It was hard to make small talk in such an atmosphere, when what everyone really wanted was an officious Romulan neck to wrap their hands around.

Sensitive to such moodiness, McCoy forced a smile and said jovially, "Well, we're still in business." He lifted his buttermilk. "And so I propose a toast to celebrate our narrow escape—is this the four hundred tenth or eleventh?"

Other drinking goblets were raised. "Cheers ... goganko ... offiah ..."

No one had managed a single sip, however, before a startled Sulu let out an exclamation of surprise. He was staring downwards, at the dark stain that now ran across the front of his uniform.

"Hey ... this glass just leaked all over me!"

The emotions running around the table were not of amusement, though. Uhura's yelp of surprise followed soon after.

"How do you like that ... so did mine?"

"And mine," Scott added.

Everyone, in fact, sported identical stains. Confusion and puzzlement reigned. An observation came first from Spock, as usual.

"It appears that we are all victims of a rather bizarre coincidence."

McCoy looked around the table. "Maybe ... maybe ..."

"The odds against this happening," Spock went on, "against all our glasses being defective or all of us being this sloppy, are astronomical."

McCoy was brushing at his drenched shirt-front and abruptly looked up. "Astronomical my metatarsals! This is no coincidence. I just remembered—we used to pull tricks like this all the time in medical school." He eyed his cup. "Dribble glasses ... we've been hit with dribble glasses." A slow survey of the table followed.

"Don't look now, but we've got a practical joker among us."

"Don't jump to conclusions, Bones," admonished Kirk. But he also found himself studying the faces of his table companions. All except Spock, of course, who was automatically above suspicion. He could not have imagined a dribble glass, much less considered employing one.

For that matter, it hardly seemed the sort of prank anyone present would pull.

"This isn't a group from which I'd expect this kind of infantile humor. Spock's probably right, Bones ... it's just an incredible coincidence."

"That's right," Sulu agreed. "We all got wet, so who'd be playing the joke?"

"Probably a minor defect in the inorganic, nonmetallic fabricator programming," Scott supplied helpfully. "I'll check it out with the specialists in charge on the next shift."

"Good enough," Kirk said with finality. "Right now, I suggest that everyone finish eating before the food gets as cold as my drink."

To set an example, he picked up a fork full of fried potatoes. But as he moved it toward his mouth, the fork suddenly wilted in the middle as if the metal had turned molten. The large helping fell in a greasy splotch down the front of his tunic. It made an interesting contrast to the stain already left by his drink.

Whether it was the awkward tumbling of solid food or the fact that this time only the captain was affected, one couldn't say; but several giggles sounded around the table. They were rapidly stifled.

McCoy hadn't joined in the chuckling. "Another coincidence, Jim?"

Kirk brushed at his shirt and gazed around the table again, more thoughtfully this time. "I'm beginning to wonder, Bones." He eyed the fork.

Something had bent the metal neatly in half midway down the stem. How, he couldn't tell. It appeared to be a perfectly ordinary fork. Close inspection failed to reveal any hidden hinge or abrasions where it might have been filed.

"I'm beginning to wonder . . ."

They finished the hexed meal in comparative silence, and without further incident. If there was a practical joker among them, he or she was abashed enough to forgo any further demonstrations.

However, the problem did not fade away. It continued to make itself felt throughout the ship . . . and in the most unexpected ways. The first new manifestation occurred following the command shift's return to the Bridge. Spock noticed an instrument lying on his console which hadn't been there when he had left. He utterly failed to recognize it. It was obvious how it was supposed to be utilized, but when he tried, he achieved nothing.

"Curious," he finally muttered, "most curious."

Kirk heard and strolled over from the navigation printout where he had been studying statistical readouts on the energy cloud.

"What is, Spock ... what've you got there?" The first officer held it out to him. It was a small tubular device, rather like a monoculor viewer.

"I found this instrument on my console, Captain. There is only this single adjustable ring to serve as any kind of control. But it does nothing ... see?"

Placing the eyepiece against his left eye, he fiddled with the ring. At the same time, Kirk noticed the dark ring encircling his right eye. When he pulled the tube away, a matching black circle had appeared around Spock's other eye—a circle, he noted, exactly the same size and shape as the eyepiece.

"It appears to serve no useful function," Spock added. "My best efforts have failed to produce any noticeable result."

In spite of himself, Kirk laughed. So did Sulu and Uhura when they turned and saw the result.

Spock simply stood there, befuddled, glancing from the comm station, to the helm and back to Kirk. Naturally, his ignorance of the situation made it all the funnier to the onlookers.

"I'm ... sorry, Spock," Kirk finally managed to gasp, getting himself under control. "You see, you . . ." He couldn't manage to produce a quiet explanation. Instead, he pantomimed circles around his own eyes.

Spock continued to stand there for a moment, considering this nonverbal information carefully. Then he reached up and dabbed at his face with one hand. When he brought his fingers down, the tips of two were covered with black smudge.

His lips didn't twist, but he succeeded in scowling with his eyebrows . . .

If that had been the last incident, Kirk might still have put it down to someone's idea of humor. But the "incidents," as everyone on board was soon calling them, occurred with increasing frequency. And they became less and less amusing.

Only serious thoughts filled Scott's mind as he strolled down the corridor leading back to Engineering Central. Final repairs on the damage wrought by the Romulans were nearing completion, but a few delicate adjustments still had to be made in certain heavily battered sections.

Intricate repairs required careful thought, which in turn engendered a profound hunger. He paused by one of the galley annexes, just as Arex and M'ress rounded the far corner, walking in the opposite direction.

"Officer Scott," Arex called, "if you're hungry, won't you join us for lunch. We were just on our way to mess." His soulful visage radiated friendliness.

Scott politely declined. "No thanks, Arex. I'm just goin' to grab a bit of a snack before I get back to my work. I kinna afford to let some of my younger techs alone too long with certain machinery." He grinned.

"As it will go," Arex replied amiably. "Any word on who was responsible for the ... dribble glasses, someone called them, and for what happened to First Officer Spock?"

"Not a clue. And I've heard scuttlebutt about a number of other childish pranks having taken place around the ship."

Arex and M'ress exchanged glances. "We haven't hearrd anything, orr seen anything like that," M'ress purred.

"Maybe you're immune ... lucky you."

"I hope so, consideirring what happened to Mrr. Spock," M'ress replied feelingly. *"Mm-aorrr ... how embarrassing!"*

"See you later," Arex added, as they continued on down the corridor.

Scott murmured a goodbye, then activated the console. Identifying himself as to name and rank, he absently ordered a grilled Swiss cheese on rye.

"No ... make that pumpernickel," he corrected quickly. The ACKNOWLEDGE light came on promptly. Scott pressed the second button, was rewarded by the sight of a filled plate slipping into place behind the transparent receiver guard.

Reaching in, he removed the sandwich, then turned to leave. As he did so, there was a second muffled thump behind him.

Puzzled, he looked back. A second sandwich had appeared in the opening. He shrugged and withdrew it ... only to see it instantly replaced by yet another ... and that by two, piled atop one another.

Muttering to himself, he set his three on the floor and removed the two new ones. Two more appeared, followed by another three ... the last made with Limburger cheese instead of Swiss.

These were replaced by, in rapidly accelerating order, wedges of fudge cake, linzer torte, falafel, three steaming bowls of chop suey, blacktop sundaes, and a dismembered, smoked turkey.

Blinking and whining like a ratchet wrench with the colic, the machine started to flush a river of food so fast Scott had no time for culinary classification.

"What the blazes ... *hold it a minute!*"

His hands were already covered with cheese, melting ice cream, and sauces of various composition and ethnic origin. The lower half of his uniform was splattered.

"I said *one sandwich!*" he shouted frantically. "One blasted sandwich, ye great glob of gastronomical gadgetry!"

Footsteps sounded in the corridor. Arex and M'ress reappeared, on the run. "Mr. Scott," Arex called, "we heard yelling. Is everything ... ?" The concerned piping of the Edoan navigator stopped abruptly. Next to him, M'ress had commenced a smooth, feline laugh. Arex joined her.

"I'm sorry, Officer Scott," he gasped. "Excuse us, but ..."

"Go ahead and laugh, go on ... big joke!" Scott muttered in irritation as he warded off a barrage of burritos and kidney pie. "I'll wager you two are responsible for everything that ... hey!"

The console was ejecting food through the input/recycle slot now, doubling its firepower and making it harder for him to grab at the control panel—even though various stabs and punches at said switches had failed to produce any lessening of the comestible bombardment.

"Just a moment, Officer Scott," Arex objected, his laughter dying down. "We're not responsible for this or any of the other reported pranks. How could I program this? I have no idea if half of the ... dishes ... lying about are even edible."

"It could be a random program," Scott countered. "I wonder if the captain will buy your excuse."

He dodged a stream of curried kooftah a Persian gourmet would have been proud of and took another step toward the controls. If he could just unbolt the master panel, he could bypass the circuitry and ...

"I'm reportin' the both of ye as soon as I ..." He paused as he reached the wall, bent to touch the first of two screw latches near the floor.

As he did so a large cream pie shot with impressive velocity out of the machine and caught him flush in the face, knocking him backward several steps. He recovered his balance and stood there, wiping whipped cream from his eyes and staring blankly at the machine.

"Believe us, Officer Scott," Arex began seriously, "we have nothing to do with ... ," but the chief engineer ignored him, backing away from the annex as if it had suddenly acquired a malevolent intelligence of its own.

That last pie had been thrown *hard*—and aimed.

He eyed the machine warily.

That was not to be the last of the strange occurrences to plague the ship.

VI

The pranks multiplied, accompanied by a corresponding decrease in subtlety. Finally it reached the point where even the ship's repairs were being interfered with. The apogee of absurdity was reached when a glowering Kirk came stomping onto the Bridge to stand, hands on hips, just inside the elevator portal.

Arex turned from the navigation console and Spock from his library computer station while M'ress glanced across from communications. "Okay," Kirk announced in a no-nonsense, anything-but-amused voice, "this whole thing has gone far enough."

There were equal parts frustration and anger in his tone. This sudden fury was unlike the captain. Everyone stared at him, baffled.

"What has . . . sir?" Arex finally ventured.

Kirk bestowed a baleful glare on the innocent navigator. "I just picked up my clean uniforms from the service chute, Mr. Arex. When I put one on, I discovered *this*." He turned his back to them.

Lettered across the back of his shirt, in bold yellow, were the words: KIRK IS A JERK.

Below this someone had stenciled a simplistic childlike face with crossed eyes and a silly grin.

Events aboard had progressed to the point where no one was surprised at *any* kind of report. But this blatant assault on Kirk's position produced astonished stares from the Bridge personnel. It had progressed from flat humor to outright insult.

There was a brief, startled giggle from somewhere. Everyone looked nervously at his neighbor, but the giggle was not repeated. It had been indeterminate as to source or gender—fortunately for the giggler.

Everyone was sure of one thing. *They* hadn't laughed—and each in his own way tried to convey that information wordlessly to Kirk as he examined each one in turn. "When the outburst of hysteria has concluded, I'd like an explanation for this recent burst of puerility."

"That," suggested Spock in a strange tone of voice, "may be more difficult than it seems. I was watching both Lieutenant Arex and Lieutenant M'ress closely. I saw no one laugh. Needless to say," he finished quietly, "it did not come from me."

"Someone certainly laughed," Kirk countered, his anger dying as curiosity took over.

Further discussion was interrupted as M'ress suddenly rose from her chair to point past Kirk. "Captain, look behind you."

"Really, M'ress," a thoroughly fed-up Kirk muttered, "you're going to have to be more clever than that."

"It's not a joke, sir," Arex confirmed.

Kirk whirled . . . and took a couple of steps backward. A thick clinging fog was billowing inward from the turbolift shaft. It swirled around his legs, hugging the floor.

"Now what?"

Spock was preparing an answer. The computer supplied it readily. "The source of the atmospheric aberration appears to be centralized two decks below, Captain."

Fog or not, the lift operated efficiently. When Kirk pressed the emergency-stop switch and the door slid aside, it was to reveal a corridor filled from deck to ceiling with a roiling, eerie mist.

Spock took two steps into the cloud and stopped, pulling a small sensorscan from his hip. He took readings and measurements while Kirk fidgeted nervously behind him.

"Well?"

"Frankly, I had expected something else, Captain," he replied, without going into specifics on what the "something else" might be, "but this appears to be a normal, everyday water-based fog ... except that such occurrences are *not* normal on a starship. Perhaps the humidification monitors are—"

Taking another step forward, he began flailing wildly as his legs started out from under him. He twisted and fought for balance with inhuman control. Kirk moved quickly to grab him—then found himself slipping and sliding as though on bearings. But by using one another for support and finally struggling to the projections on a nearby door, they were able to avoid a serious fall. After regaining their balance, it took a bit longer to catch their breath.

That accomplished, Spock disdained the sensorscan for less detailed but more immediate methods of study. He knelt carefully. Nearness to the source of the trouble brought revelation.

"Amazing," he murmured. "The deck here is covered with ice."

"It was almost covered with us," Kirk rumbled. "What kind of ice, Spock?"

"From all indications, normal water ice, Captain. It does not appear to possess exotic or dangerous properties ... beyond the obvious physical ones, of course."

"Ice," Kirk said, staring down the corridor into the frosty miasma. "I don't know what's happening on this ship, Mr. Spock, but it's got to stop before somebody gets hurt. Whoever's responsible for this is getting carried away with his own inventiveness."

As if on cue, the strange giggle was heard again. Kirk had no need to look around for possible concealed bodies—he and Spock were alone in the corridor. That annoying giggle was loud and distinct this time. In fact, it was faintly feminine and almost—almost familiar.

Kirk took a step toward what he thought might be the source of the sound. Was someone hiding in that fog after all? Instantly he found himself sliding crazily. Only Spock's firm grip enabled him to recover his balance again.

"That laugh—it sounds very much like the one I thought I heard on the Bridge a few minutes ago.

There's something awfully familiar about it." He eyed his first. "What do you make of all this, Spock?"

"Despite the increasing number of incidents, Captain, the evidence seems to point to a single guilty party."

"How do you know it's not sev—" Kirk's eyes widened. "You think you know who it is, don't you?"

"Not who, Captain—what. I believe that our practical joker is the *Enterprise* herself."

"The *Enterprise* ... ?" Kirk hesitated, mulled the hypothesis over in his head. Then familiarity and fact came together, and everything else fell into place.

"Everything makes sense now. That carefully calculated feminine tone—it's the voice of our main computer!"

"Precisely," Spock agreed.

"I want all hands to stations, all computer techs to work doubleshift. We're going to run a complete cybernetics systems-check from bow to stern and get to the bottom of this." His voice grew threatening.

"Trick glasses and offensive food-processing equipment is one thing. But when some circuit failure starts affecting the ship's programming ..."

"I heartily concur, Captain. This must be stopped before these pranks grow any more serious.

"At the moment, though, we have a less lethal if more immediate problem." He used his eyes to indicate the floor behind them. "Getting from here to the lift again in one piece, since the floor is now frozen over behind us."

There is no problem, however, that is ultimately insoluble under assault from the combined abilities of a Federation cruiser captain and his science officer. Crawling carefully on hands and knees, they made their way safely back to the elevator.

While Arex and M'ress handled their duties forward and Kirk and Spock pondered the problem posed by the apparent breakdown of the central computer, an off-duty Uhura and Sulu were approaching the main door to the Recreation Room. McCoy joined them a moment later.

Uhura touched the switch beside the door latch. A small transparent indicator lit up in green with the word UNOCCUPIED. They followed a small beep provided for the benefit of color-blind, non-Anglo-reading personnel and guests.

Uhura fairly purred with satisfaction. "Good; nobody home ... at least we can enjoy our free time without worrying about practical jokes."

The heavy door slid aside. McCoy trailed them in. "Exactly what the doctor ordered," he quipped, taking in the restful (if illusory) scene of park grounds and fountains.

"The standard re-creation," Sulu observed. "Now for something a bit more original and relaxing." He activated the control which shut the door behind them, closing them off from the rest of the ship.

A moment later an electronic chime struck three times, and Spock's voice filled the empty corridor as it did every chamber and walkway aboard.

"All hands to your stations—this is a general alert. Repeat, all hands to your stations. Second and third computer shifts, report to briefing, second and third computer shifts, report to briefing. Repeat, all hands to sta—"

But within the sealed environment of the Recreation Room, the order went unheard. Possibly something was wrong with the inside intercom speakers.

Possibly ...

Sulu moved to the only visible sign of electronic presence in the big room. This isolated fixture was a small console located to the right of the main door. He proceeded to activate it, clearing the park scene from the room.

They stood in the chamber as it actually was, now—a vast hall with distant, curving walls. Ceilings, walls, deck were a uniform malleable white. It was like standing inside a smooth ivory dome.

"Something soothing and homey," the helmsman murmured with anticipation. "What'll it be?" he asked his companions. "Anyone object to a swim at the beach?"

Sulu turned his attention to the intricate keyboard

and display screen mounted above. A detailed, three-dimensional schematic of the room program would appear there as the console operator designed it. The console itself consisted of a standard keyboard, plus numerous other controls for adjusting such things as climate, time of day, special effects—and many more. Sulu keyed the latter—only officers and qualified enlisted personnel were permitted to manipulate such touchy details as temperature and oxygen content.

As he worked the dials and switches and buttons, an image gradually began to form on the screen. Minutes passed. As helmsman, Sulu was especially adept in handling computer controls. The diagram formed rapidly under his skillful touch.

Eventually Sulu paused to study the picture, pressed another switch to add a little peripheral vegetation, and examined the finished program with pleasure. He touched another switch and the diagram rotated three hundred and sixty degrees, then displayed itself on an angle.

With a little flourish he keyed the INITIATE switch.

Around them, above them, below them, the room began to change.

Spock would have described it as a routine readjustment of physical conditions within a confined space produced by the recreational computer-annex drawing on the extensive fabrication facilities of the *Enterprise*. Anyone born over a couple of hundred years before would have called it a miracle.

But then, Spock could redefine that in simple, logical terms as well.

This design facility was primitive compared to the master dream computer they'd encountered on another world,* but within its limits it was capable of some very effective transmutations in the interest of alleviating shipboard tedium.

Shimmering, fluorescent forms took on substance and the illusion of solidity. Walls and ceilings vanished—to be replaced by a sandy seashore, complete with lapping wavelets and the distant call of gulls. The

*See "Once upon a Planet," *Star Trek Log Three*.

recreation annex wasn't up to producing three-dimensional simulacra of the birds themselves. That was too fluid an illusion to maintain. But three-dimensional projections of sea birds were available and they flashed on the distant deep-blue sky.

Sulu paid attention to details—after all, advanced manipulation of such instrumentation was an art form. A starfish hugged the water's edge here, dried kelp encrusted the sloping berm there.

"Nice job, Sulu," McCoy complimented, assessing the finalized creation. "You handle water well, but personally this is kind of hot for me. I'm more in the mood for a nice, quiet stroll in the woods."

"That sounds perfect, Doctor," Uhura admitted, squinting up to where a powerful light source reposed in placid imitation of a sun.

"Why didn't you say so?" Sulu asked agreeably. "Woods it is then . . . dark and deep."

A single touch dissolved water, gulls, sand, starfish and kelp. The helmsman began again from scratch.

Botany was a favorite hobby of his. As such, he was able to create an even better simulacrum of McCoy's request than he had of the beach. The forest he conjured up (deciduous, North American, temperate zone) was lush and seemingly endless. Rays of sunlight fell like wax blades through the branches and illumined shifting motes of dust. It was a fulfilled vision, even to the moss on the "north" side of the trees and the appropriate fungal undergrowth.

"Ahhh . . . that's more like it," McCoy complemented, savoring the crispness in the air and breathing deeply of the aroma of pine and birch . . . artificial through it might be. He made an after-you gesture and followed Uhura and Sulu as they started off down the path between the trees.

Their course would wind around and through the limited confines of the recreation chamber. If they got bored, a few touches on the console—now discreetly concealed by Sulu behind a young maple—would alter the terrain yet again. Meanwhile they enjoyed the cool, faint dampness of their own personal forest and tried to identify Sulu's purposely jumbled, programmed bird calls . . .

M'ress, running through the acknowledgments from key personnel which was standard procedure during a general alert, noticed the failure of three officers to report in. She double-checked before bringing the matter to Kirk's attention.

"Captain," she finally reported, "accorrding to elimination prrocedurre and last eye-witness accounts, officerrs McCoy, Sulu, and Uhurra arre still in the main rrecrreation rroom. They have failed eitherr to rrespond to orr to acknowledge the call to stations."

"That's not necessarily surprising, Lieutenant," Kirk said easily. "To maintain lengthy illusions the main recreation room can be total-sealed from the rest of the ship. You can probably reach them by patching through to the rec room's own speaker system."

"That's just it, sirr, I've alrready *trried* that." She sounded worried. "They still fail to rrespond. I can't even tell if the call is going thrrough."

Kirk stiffened in his chair. "Now that *is* surprising. Try once more."

M'ress turned back to her console, activated the necessary bypasses and overrides. "Drr. McCoy, Lieutenant Uhurra, Lieutenant Sulu . . . returrn to the Brridge immediately. This is a generral alarrm. I rrepeat, a generral alarrm. Please acknowledge."

"Again," Kirk ordered tightly. What was going on?

M'ress sighed, raised her voice even though she knew the pick-up would compensate automatically. "Drr. McCoy, Lieutenant Uhurra, Lieutenant Sulu . . . rreturrn to the Brrid . . ."

The path through the closely packed, tall trees was bordered with thick patches of ferns. Water dripped from a high place into a bog where a venus flytrap closed over the projection of an ant.

The faintly metallic ping of water falling into a small pond was the only sound in the solitude of the forest. The three strollers entered a glade lined with high ferns and brightly colored mushrooms and toadstools. Bark fungi formed elf ladders in the trees.

"So quiet, so relaxing," Sulu murmured. "Such a change from orders and routine. An excellent selection, Doctor."

"Me for a short snooze," Uhura declared, heading for the shade of a thick maple.

"And best of all, no practical jokes," McCoy exclaimed. "Unless," he added half-jokingly, "one of you is the dearly-sought culprit."

Sulu sat down on the grass and grinned. The grin vanished as an unnatural, distant giggle broke the stillness. Uhura looked up curiously from where she'd just gotten comfortable. McCoy was scanning the sky and surrounding trees.

"I know you're especially good at animal detail, Sulu ... but this doesn't strike me as an Irish enough a landscape to qualify for leprechauns."

"That wasn't anything I programmed," Sulu informed him. He was inspecting the dark underbrush with some concern. The illusion inventory of the rec annex was pretty extensive. If someone wanted to give them a scare by introducing a Taurean scimitar-wolf, now ...

"Almost sounded like someone chuckling."

The giggle—if that's what it was—wasn't repeated. McCoy finally shrugged. "Probably just a malfunction in one of the audio-effects tapes. Maybe a rewind blotch mixed in with the forward play ... could be most anything. We're all a bit jumpy from the stories circulating."

Uhura climbed to her feet. The glade no longer seemed quite so inviting. "I think I'll pass on that nap. Besides, I'm not that tired yet."

They crossed the open patch of green, picked up the dirt path on the far side. It disappeared ahead and veered to the left among the trees.

Around that first bend, the path unexpectedly vanished. A large square hole intersected its course. As if coaxed by an argumentative breeze, branches appeared from the undergrowth and arranged themselves with unnatural precision across the gap. Once this latticework was complete, leaves and pine needles fell from above and masked the intertwined branches.

They continued to drift downward until even so astute an observer as Spock would have been unable to tell that only a smattering of dead leaves and twigs covered the hole in the pathway. A last leaf, an afterthought, slipped into place to conceal a tiny hint of darkness as McCoy, Sulu and Uhura appeared in the distance, admiring the scenery and landscape ahead.

None of them heard the unnatural yet familiar highpitched giggling that sounded in that part of the forest. It was concealed by something by now expert at concealment.

"That's a hemlock, isn't it, Sulu?" McCoy asked, pointing at a tall, handsome growth. "Beautiful. I liked your beach, but ... ," he gestured expansively, "I wanted something a bit more closed and cooling. It's almost as if ... *hey!*"

His exclamation was matched by a startled yelp from Sulu and a scream from Uhura. This was followed instantly by some ungentle flopping sounds. A rustle of broken leaves and crushed twigs, and then all was quiet.

Quiet until a blast of all-pervasive giggling suddenly erupted around them. Three pairs of eyes turned nervously upwards.

But still nothing was to be seen. "That laughter again," Sulu murmured. "It wasn't our imagination."

McCoy sounded grim. "I was wrong. That's no tape malfunction. Someone's definitely laughing at us." He scrambled to his feet, wiping dirt and clinging splinters from his uniform.

"So we didn't lose our practical joker by coming here after all. But how the devil can someone hide in a cleared rec room? There aren't any sharp corners or dips to hide behind."

"There's an emergency override on the doorseal," Sulu recalled. "Someone might have entered after we'd established this simulacrum."

"Possible," McCoy agreed. "Everyone all right?"

Uhura was just getting to her feet. She winced slightly as she put pressure on her left ankle, but nodded. Sulu had fallen with the practice of one who reacts to such tumbles instinctively. He was unharmed and unbruised. McCoy had simply been lucky.

"Okay." The doctor glanced upward. "I don't know about you two, but I've had enough. I'm going to get to the bottom of this right now!" His statement provoked a response as unexpected as it was rapid. A barrage of giggles preceded an oddly stilted voice that chuckled, "Get to the *bottom* of this." The kibbitzer's tone was jovial, but it did nothing to improve McCoy's dampened humor. He pointed upward, aiming for a spiritual target in the absence of a physical one.

"All right, whoever you are. We fell for your idiotic little joke. Now get us out of here."

"*Fell* for my joke," the voice echoed, evidently entranced with its own wit. "*Fell* for . . . ," it dissolved in burbling chuckles.

Ordinarily, one if not all of the imprisoned officers would have identified the source of that voice by now. But their memories were temporarily clouded by a combination of anger and disgust. They could still only conceive of a flesh and blood antagonist.

"When we find out who you are," McCoy continued furiously, "you're going to be called on the deck before a board of inquiry . . . you can bet on it."

Such threats produced no lapse in the steady flow of laughter. On the contrary, it seemed to increase in proportion to the severity of the threat.

"I'm warning you," Sulu added, "the captain will bust you, whoever you are. This has gone far enough. It's not funny any more . . . not that any of these pranks ever were."

More giggles . . . their unseen adversary appeared to have an unlimited capacity for laughter.

McCoy looked at his companions. "It seems obvious that whoever we're arguing with is too smitten with his own humor to listen to reason—much less to lend us a hand. We'll have to dig our way out of this."

Turning, McCoy tested the composition of the pit wall. The artificial soil was soft and crumbly. He let his gaze travel to the lip of the depression. The hole they found themselves in—no doubt that thought would

amuse their unbalanced prankster if he were to voice
it—was not terribly deep. But the four walls were vertical. No human ladder, then, and no climbing straight
up.

Experimentally, he dug at the dirt. It came away
easily.

"Maybe too easily, Doctor," suggested a worried
Uhura. "We don't want any sudden cave-ins."

McCoy looked doubtful. "Oh, I don't think our
jokester would let it go that far. Besides," he added
sardonically, "if we're killed, how could we be the
butt of any more jokes? In any case, I don't intend to
sit around waiting for him to decide. Want to give me a
hand?"

Working together they tried to cut a sloping path out
of the pit, occasionally having to back off quickly when
a handful brought the dirt above it sliding down. They
rapidly became filthy. No sign of a cave-in appeared. It
was a slow, monotonous job, but they'd be out before
long. As McCoy had supposed, their unseen tormentor
showed no inclination to offer assistance.

Spock finally looked up from his console to find an
anxious Kirk staring at him, waiting for information.
"Sorry, Captain . . . nothing. I've tried re-patching
around the apparently defective emergency override,
and canceling out any present programming, without
result."

"Ample evidence exists to show that they are still inside, however. Someone's oxygen is being recycled, and
from time to time power is still being drawn to operate
the simulacrum machinery.

"Which leaves us with two possibilities," Kirk
finished. "Either they can't respond—for what reason
we don't know yet. Or else equipment malfunction is
preventing them from even trying to answer." The
command chair hummed softly as it swung round.

"M'ress . . . any luck yet?"

"Still no rresponse thrrough any channels, Captain."

Kirk pondered. "Let's go to the source on this,
Spock. It's the computer that's been giving us trouble.

The computer supervises everything that goes on in that rec room. So . . ."

"I was about to suggest that myself, Captain."

Spock turned, and his fingers began a lithe, precise dance over the ship's instrumentation. The blink of indicator lights and the compliant hums and beeps of responsive equipment followed. The reply was presented both in printed form on Spock's screens, and aurally over the Bridge speakers.

"That is for me to know and for you to find out," it announced.

Spock's eyebrows looked as if they had crawled clear up his forehead, through his hair and down his rear collar. Infantile riddle-replies he'd come to expect occasionally from humans. But that something as precise and coldly logical as the ship's computer might resort to such barbaric foolishness seemed to all but herald the end of reason.

Kirk's reaction was nearly as incredulous. "Did I hear that right, Mr. Spock?" he mumbled in astonishment.

"I am afraid," Spock said slowly, "that you did, Captain. The malfunction is clearly more severe than I believed possible." He returned his attention to his keyboard.

"Question," he inquired carefully. "Are you deliberately holding Dr. McCoy, and Lieutenants Uhura and Sulu captive in the main recreation room?"

Another prompt response, this time with a subtle alteration that hinted, perhaps, at something less than complete control over its disturbed circuitry. Certainly, Kirk mused, it wouldn't *want* to sound like a petulant child.

"I'll never tell," it whined. "Never ever never. Can't make me, either. Can't, can't, *can't!* And I won't."

Hands clenched tightly, Kirk rose and walked over to stand by Spock. "Let me try," he whispered, then directed his voice to the input pickup.

"This is Captain James T. Kirk speaking," he announced with as much steel in his voice he could muster. "You are programmed to obey any direct order I may give."

"That is correct," the voice replied evenly.

Some of Kirk's fury abated at that conciliatory response. Maybe what the computer needed to break it free of this inexplicable insanity was just a little drill-sergeant firmness. Slowly, he continued.

"Very well ... I order you to release officers McCoy, Sulu and Uhura from the recreation chamber *immediately*."

A series of flashes and winks from the console, followed by a gentle query, "Say 'please?' "

"Well I'll be!" Kirk gulped, by now beyond amazement. Spock leaned back to murmur.

"One should not debate command priority with a machine, Captain. Under the circumstances, I would suggest compliance coupled with a temporary swallowing of pride."

Kirk started to object, then nodded slowly. Keeping his voice level with an effort, he murmured, "Please?"

A quiet pause, and this time the indicator lights seemed to flash in more natural sequence. He was about to exchange a glance of triumph with Spock when the voice jumped in with gleeful clarity, "Say 'pretty please' ..."

Kirk snapped off the audio control before any further taunts could be offered. Arex appeared about to say something, thought better of it as Kirk switched the main viewscreen into the intercom system. A terse call and the result was an image of a concerned engineer Scott to go along with his voice.

"Mr. Scott, I've had it up to here."

"Aye, Captain," Scott concurred, ignoring Kirk's angry tone. He could guess its source. Elaboration was sure to follow.

He was right. "We've got some serious trouble with the main computer, Scotty. It's not just custard pies and slippery decks, now. We're pretty sure it's kidnapped Dr. McCoy, Sulu, and Uhura."

"Kidnapped ... the main computer?" Scott's lined face underwent a series of highland contortions as the import of Kirk's words penetrated. "The main computer ... but how ...?"

"We're not sure yet."

Scott considered. "Why not ask it to explain itself?"

"We've tried that Scotty." Kirk smiled tightly. "All we've got in reply are taunts and nonsense. Neither Mr. Spock nor myself think continuing along that line is going to produce any useful result—and it doesn't do anything for my blood pressure, either. I can see only one solution, one chance of forestalling even more serious trouble." He sighed.

"I want you to shut down all higher logic functions until we can get *some* kind of handle on what's responsible for perpetrating this cybernetic imbecility."

"Aye, sir," Scott replied, coming to attention verbally.

"Leave only the purely supportive circuitry operational," Kirk went on. "I want everything capable of abstract reasoning and creative cognition put out of commission until we can get a crew in the central core to dissect those information banks. We can't risk further mismanipulation of on-board functions."

"I'll get a crew right on it, sir. And I'll handle the main lobotomy myself. Scott out."

"Bridge out." Kirk switched off. Scott's image disappeared, leaving the captain confronted with a panorama of alien constellations.

VII

Another double handful of soil, yet another . . . and then the last. Sulu stepped back and took stock of the steep incline they had cut in the pit wall.

"I think that'll do it, Uhura." He smiled expectantly. "Ready?"

She took a deep breath. "I haven't done any serious climbing in years." In her Academy days, she and several daring friends had ascended the Aeolian Pyre on Tsavo II. If they could see the worry she was expressing now, over mounting ten feet of dirt, they would laugh.

Sulu and McCoy formed a double support with interlocked hands. With this boost, and moving carefully so as not to dislodge any more dirt, she was able to scramble over the rim.

The helmsman followed her a moment later. Then it was their turn to aid a less agile McCoy as he, struggling and cursing, fought his way to the top of the incline.

"When I get my hands on the clown who's behind this," he vowed, panting heavily, "I'll put him in Sick Bay for a month!"

Sulu rocked back on his heels and mopped at his sweaty face. "I thought you were supposed to operate the other way around, Dr. McCoy?"

"This is one time," McCoy countered, "where I think I'd enjoy drumming up some of my own business."

He would have added more, but the forest surrounding them chose that moment to flicker into chaos. Before anyone thought to inquire aloud what was happening, the tall, temperate grove with its gentle breeze and scented air had been replaced by a howling wilderness of ice and snow. Gale winds laden with snow and tiny, stinging ice chips lashed at them, while above the bone-chilling wind an admonishing voice cried, "Temper, temper! Perhaps this will cool you off!"

Huddled together for warmth, the three officers tried to take stock of their new environment while shielding their faces with cupped hands. Attempting to ignore the driving cold, Sulu made a slow turn. No matter which way he looked there was nothing to be seen but white ground and whiter sky. "We've got a regular blizzard condition here . . . how are we ever going to find the exit?"

McCoy was stamping his feet. The surface shrank from the irregular friction . . . it was real snow, all right.

Giggles fell like snowflakes around them as the temperature plunged to arctic levels . . .

Scott was still trying to imagine how the computer had effected the "kidnapping" of his friends. The abduction puzzled him, the more so since a harried Kirk had not seen fit—or perhaps felt he hadn't the time—to explain the rec room situation.

Future speculation, he decided, would have to wait until he'd carried out the captain's command.

He turned a corner and confronted a sealed single door. He pressed his thumb to the sensor square below the stenciled lettered which spelled, "WARNING—AUTHORIZED PERSONNEL ONLY".

At the moment the main computer room was empty. Since this central cortex rarely required servicing and was kept sealed in all but critical situations, it hadn't been visited recently by anyone except the standard security patrol. His practiced gaze showed no hint of unauthorized activity.

This isolation was a pity, since in its fashion the central computer cortex was one of the more impressive sights on the ship. Bank on bank of tireless indicator lights, liquid crystal displays, glowing poured circuitry—

and all this only the tiny, visible part of the ship's heart and brain.

His destination lay at the far end of the room. There he was required to supply his thumbprint again, not to mention having to present both eyes for a retinal identification check. Only then would a hitherto hidden slot present itself for the offer of a special key card. Insertion of the key caused a broad, man-high panel to click and then slide silently aside, revealing a series of sequential switches and controls mounted over a color-coded keyboard.

Human memory activated mechanical as he tapped out a rarely used combination. This caused several sets of the sequential controls mounted above to glow . . . the higher logic and creative reasoning telltales. These were subdivided in turn into various sections embossed with such headings as *Intuitive Reasoning, Abstraction, Deduction,* and *Stage IV Response.* The unlit sections he ignored. "Time for a nap, old girl," he murmured. "Captain's orders." His hand moved for the first of the red-colored switches.

He never reached it.

A piercing whine filled the chamber. It soared into could feel more than a momentary pain. Total disorientation set in as he strove to readjust himself to the fact that he was tumbling toward the ceiling. He landed there with a thud, flat on his back.

Typically, his initial reaction was more emotional than effective. Once he managed to regain his balance and force his mind to accept the fact he wasn't going to plunge to the floor, he rolled over and crawled above the upside-down console set in the far wall.

"Engineering to Bridge," he bawled over the barely reachable intercom. "I've got a problem down here, sir."

Kirk was able to offer commiseration if not help. Exactly the same situation prevailed on the Bridge, where he, Spock, and everyone else had been similarly thrown to the roof.

Spock managed to activate the main intercom by

crawling up his library-computer console—or was he crawling down?

"Scotty, what the blazes is going on?"

"I'm not sure, Captain." He tested himself carefully and with self-control only an experienced spacer could the range of imperceptible ultrasonics before Scott muster, walked across the ceiling toward the next bank of interdeck monitors. A quick check was enough to show him that his personal plight was being repeated on every level.

"Our gravity's reversed polarity—all by itself, it seems."

"The latter conclusion is an obvious falsehood," came Spock's clear voice. He was sitting upside-down in his seat, studying the information displayed on his readouts. "This is an undeniable defensive maneuver by the computer, to prevent Mr. Scott from disconnecting its higher functions."

"Crazy," Kirk muttered, "this is crazy. Not jokes anymore. Our own computer's declared war on us . . . and I haven't the slightest idea why."

"I do not believe the term 'war' is yet applicable to this situation, Captain. The computer has not yet shown itself to be openly antagonistic—only misguidedly self-centered." He looked thoughtful, relaxed despite his upside-down position. "I do have a theory; but first I suggest that if Officer Scott moved away from the computer's logic terminal—far away—it might feel less threatened, and therefore less inclined to take direct action against us."

"Threatened? Mr. Spock, that computer is programmed with so many stabilizing circuits . . ." His objections were halted by the look on his first officer's face.

"All right," he murmured in resignation, "never argue with reality, I suppose." He directed his voice toward the intercom. "Mr. Scott . . . vacate the computer room."

Scott's eyes widened at the order. "Vacate, sir? Now, after this?" His gaze strayed longingly towards the still uncovered terminal.

"On the double, Mr. Scott."

"Aye, sir," he sighed. For a brief moment he considered making a dash for the lobotomizing controls—

then he decided against it. Not because of what Kirk might say, but because if threatened again the crazed computer might resort to an even more severe distortion of ecological controls. He couldn't risk exposing anyone but himself to danger more severe than a bad tumble.

Unable to insure that only he would be the object of the machine's retaliation, he turned and walked across the ceiling toward the chamber exit. He paused there for a last look backward. The panel he had opened had not been shut, the telltales still shone brightly. Apparently the computer hadn't managed to find a way to close off its own emergency shutdown. That was his sole encouraging thought. Once he was outside this door, however, those switches would be effectively protected from external manipulation. Kirk's voice sounded behind him.

"Mr. Scott?"

"Just leavin', Captain." He stepped gingerly over the low hurdle formed by the door overhead and turned on the other side, to watch it slide shut behind him.

Stretching downward, he could just reach the door control. As expected, his repeated touch had no effect at all. The door remained closed tight.

Years of experience in ship situations of all types enabled him to cope with what followed.

There was an abrupt cessation of weight, and then he found himself falling. He didn't quite land like a cat, but did succeed in turning his body enough in midair so that his arms and legs—and a less mobile portion of his anatomy—took most of the impact when he hit the floor.

Others were not so fortunate. There were some injuries—sprains, a couple of broken legs, a concussion or two—but nothing fatal.

The chief engineer rolled over and sat up, rubbing at the back of his neck and shaking a fist at the closed door. "Ye bloody big scatterbrain, make up your monumental mind!"

As expected, the door and its now isolated master did not deign to reply.

Experience had also told on the Bridge, where even minor injuries were absent.

"You were right, Spock," Kirk admitted. "Once the threat to its creative reasoning functions ceased, it no longer felt compelled to take defensive action."

The question now uppermost in his mind was, what kind of offensive action might the computer eventually decide to take? But Spock had mentioned a theory. Spock's theories usually turned out to be pretty solid.

"All right, Spock, can you tell me what's happened to my ship?"

Assuming a lecturing pose, Spock began, "Evaluation of the circumstances surrounding both the disappearance of Officers McCoy, Sulu and Uhura coupled with the many previous, though less dramatic, incidents leads me to believe that my first suspicion—that some unbalanced personality on board was tampering with the computer—is false."

"Your reasons, Spock?"

"The machinations which have been carried out so far involve extremely elaborate alterations in the computer's most delicate circuitry and programming. It strikes me that such adjustments and corresponding bypasses of all emergency overrides and fail-safes are beyond the capacity of any group of individuals on board, let alone any one. They would require the facilities and knowledge present only at a major cybernetics construction/repair center.

"With one possible exception," he finished. "Chief Engineer Scott."

"And we know Scotty's not responsible. For one thing, this kind of juvenile delinquency just isn't part of his personality." Kirk looked uncertain. "If it's not due to the actions of someone on board, what then? Central computers are supposed to be fool-proof. Ours ought to shut itself down, considering what it's already done."

"I believe there is only one possible explanation left, Captain. You remember the peculiar energy field we passed through in escaping the Romulans?"

Kirk nodded as he settled back in his chair. It had resumed its familiar location on the floor instead of the ceiling. He considered Spock's words carefully.

"I will assume," the first officer continued, "that the extremely active subatomic particles of which the energy field was composed have acted upon our computer's most sensitive circuits."

"The logic and higher reasoning centers," Kirk supplied.

"Exactly. A kind of electromagnetic infection, to put it crudely. The end result appears to have been an alteration, rather than a breakdown, of the ship's cognitive facilities.

"It is still capable of intuitive reasoning, but now along infantile instead of practical lines."

"So what you're saying," Kirk ventured by way of summing up, "is that the computer, and what it controls on board—meaning just about everything—is now in the 'hands' of a clown-mind." It was an awesome threat—even though, he had to admit, nothing terribly dangerous had happened so far.

Nothing dangerous? Then what was happening to Uhura, Sulu and McCoy?

"What can we do to correct the malfunction?"

"I'm afraid I've no idea, Captain," Spock replied solemnly. "There is nothing predictable about the computer's actions, other than its unpredictability. Without a pattern, I have nothing on which to formulate a potential solution."

Sulu hugged his arms to his sides. The gesture was more psychological prop than useful action. It did nothing to alleviate his shivering.

They had managed to stumble over a snow bank. It cut off much of the biting wind, though they all knew that if the fickle mind now in control of the computer chose to alter the gale's angle of approach, it could do so any minute. So they nestled together under the white lee and hoped their tormentor would remain otherwise occupied.

He's starting to turn blue, Uhura mused in wonderment as she stared at the shaking McCoy, her own teeth rattling. Odd . . . until now she'd thought that sort of thing only happened on visitape, subtly prepared by professional makeup men. Apparently nature was equally adept at such cosmetics.

Coming as she did from a tropical climate, the temperature drop should have affected her hardest of all. Instead, she seemed to be standing it a little better than her two companions. Sulu was little better off than McCoy.

"The temperature must be twenty below, and still dropping," she observed frigidly.

"Twenty below what?" McCoy grumbled. "Are you on the standard scale or the old Fahrenheit?"

"Well, I'm on the Sulu scale," the helmsman broke in, "and on that scale it's twenty below freezing."

"Look, we're not taking a dispassionate approach to this," suggested Uhura. "No matter how it looks, no matter how radical the illusions set before us, this is still just the Recreation Room. If we travel far enough in one line, we've got to run into one of the walls. From there we ought to be able to feel our way to the door."

McCoy struggled to his feet. He had to shout for his voice to be heard above the steady howl of the wind. "I could punch all kinds of holes in that argument, Uhura, but it's the first suggestion I've heard that contains any sense. Let's move before we all turn into icicles.

"At least walking will help keep us warm. This blizzard shows no sign of letting up."

Also, though he didn't say it, it would keep them from dwelling any longer on the increasingly serious situation they found themselves in.

The doctor found himself in the lead simply by virtue of taking the first step away from their temporary refuge. As they fought their way through the whiteout, he kept those argumentative "holes" he'd casually mentioned to Uhura to himself.

There was no point in giving their invisible assailant any suggestions.

Whoever had commandeered the rec room controls could create any, absolutely any, type of environmental simulacrum. For example, a fake solid wall. Bending it slightly could keep them feeling around in circles for hours, days, all the while thinking they were traveling in a straight line toward a never-nearing exit.

They might counter that by measuring their steps, since they knew the size of the chamber. In that case, they could find themselves confronted with an infinite series of artificial walls and exits.

An exit could be found . . . found to lead only to another section of the same snowstorm. McCoy's mind grew dizzy with the possibilites. The computer *could* let them out into a reproduction of the outside corridor. He could walk to his own cabin . . . only to awake still inside the recreation room.

It was enough to drive a man mad.

He forced himself to stray from such ominous thoughts as he struggled awkwardly through the deepening drifts. So far their pernicious prankster didn't seem that far-sighted. Or that clever.

He found himself wondering if the designers of this marvelous method of electronic escape had considered its psychiatric possibilities . . .

Kirk studied the readout on the main viewscreen. So far, the deranged computer hadn't interfered with pure information storage and retrieval facilities. Probably, he mused, because it didn't think there was anything in its banks that could be utilized against it.

There were endless tomes on computer repair, on procedures for treating mislaid circuitry, even on treating the colossal machine mind for various psychological electronic traumas. But there didn't seem to be a thing on how to treat a computer whose reasoning power had been inexplicably distorted by the effects of passage through a free-space energy complex of unknown composition. That was hardly surprising, since this was the first time it had happened.

Kirk thought sardonically that they needed to pull the plug and he had no idea where the socket was.

The viewscreen shifted to internal communications channels again, replacing the universe and chromatic emanations of the field with the more prosaic features of a tired young technician. At the moment, he wore fatigue like a badge.

"Search party to Bridge—Ensign Apple reporting."

"Bridge here—the Captain speaking. Report, Ensign."

"Our sensors indicate the missing officers are still in the Recreation Room, sir. The door appears to be jammed from the other side."

A moment's consideration, then, "Hold your position, try the door from time to time, Apple. If it opens, get in there and get them out. Report immediately if there's any change in the corridor."

"Yes, sir."

Some fast switching and the face in the screen grew older, wiser.

"Engineering," Scott acknowledged. "Captain?"

"We've finally located Uhura, Bones, and Sulu. They're in the Recreation . . ." His voice dissolved in the middle of the word . . . to a chuckle!

"Sir . . . I didn't get the end of that."

Startled, Kirk coughed and tried again. "We need a full work crew, with power tools, maybe even a laser drill, to open a badly jammed door. Have them report to . . ."

In horrified fascination, he felt his facial muscles working, twisting involuntarily into a wide grin. "Report to . . . to . . ."

He collapsed in a paroxysm of laughter. Fighting, battling his own body, he gripped the arms of the command chair so hard his knuckles turned white. His head rolled back and forth as he roared at some gut-wrenching cosmic joke.

Arex, M'ress and Spock stared at him in astonishment. But it was Scott who spoke first.

"Captain . . . what's the matter, sir? I don't understand what's . . . what's . . ."

The chief engineer of the endangered ship snorted. Then he smirked. The smirk spread to a smile broken by giggles, then chuckles—and finally he, too, was bellowing with laughter.

M'ress was the next to surrender to the assault of merriment. Her throaty, feline giggles were in sharp contrast to the deeper laughs of Kirk and Scott. She was soon joined by the weird, amused piping of Arex.

Only Spock remained silent, though not unaffected. His concern grew rapidly as he studied his out-of-control companions, while unprovoked, unrestrained hilarity reigned on the Bridge. He was about to voice an observation when both hands suddenly flew to his temples. His brows drew together in an expression of shooting pain. There was nothing he could have done to mitigate the half-anticipated attack of migraine.

Still blubbering uncontrollably, Kirk finally noticed his first officer's silence and painful grimace.

"Come on, Spock," he managed to gasp, "where's that famous Vulcan sense of humor?" This apparent apex of jocularity caused Arex and M'ress to laugh even harder. Meanwhile on the viewscreen, Scott was fighting unsuccessfully to remain in focus.

Holding one hand to the side of his head and gritting his teeth occasionally, Spock turned his attention to his computer console. The crew still retained some control over certain localized monitoring equipment, facilities the central computer apparently disdained to trouble with. Spock already suspected what had happened. Environmental analysis quickly confirmed his suspicions.

"Just as I thought," he murmured painfully.

"What are you," Arex whistled heartily, "mumbling about, Mr. Spock?"

"The atmosphere on the Bridge and presumably also in Engineering," he replied tautly, "is being pumped full of nitrous oxide, better know in the human vernacular as laughing gas. I cannot yet tell what other decks have been affected by this aerobic alteration. In any case, it is no laughing matter." His other hand darted up from the console to press at his opposite temple. "Especially for Vulcans. Breathing nitrous oxide causes . . . severe headache."

The same somber amusement was prevalent in another part of the ship, though with even grimmer overtones.

"This blizzard," Uhura roared under the effect of the gas, "keeps getting worse. And I think the temperature is still dropping.

"I know!" Sulu shouted, in forced hysteria. "If we don't keep moving, we're going to freeze to death."

McCoy fell to the snow. Already his feet and ankles were becoming numb from the unrelenting cold and damp. Nevertheless, he rolled and flailed about as if Sulu's observation were the funniest thing he'd heard in ages.

Such laughter-induced helplessness was worsening on the Bridge. Only one person was not similarly enraptured. Though in considerable pain, he was still capable of coherent thought, of responsive action.

Spock's skull felt as if it were about to fly from his shoulders. He staggered over to the engineering console. By now the pain had reached the point where it occasionally blocked out sight. But he was able to locate and adjust the necessary controls.

There was a sudden loud hum as rarely used circuits were engaged. The controls Spock had adjusted were purely manual and required no switching through any computer annex.

As a refreshing breeze flowed over them, the rest of the Bridge crew began to return to their senses, the laughter dying slowly and agonizingly.

"Thanks, Spock," Kirk was finally able to whisper, as a last chuckle forced its way loose. "How long have we got?"

Spock checked the gauges on the panel, rubbing at his head. The marching on top had ceased. "The emergency air supply should be adequate for another six hours, Captain. When that's exhausted, we'll automatically go back to standard recycled air until the emergency supply can be cleaned and retanked—assuming that's likely to take place. I would not like to comment on the odds."

"Six hours ... then we've from now till oh-eight-hundred to find a cure for the computer. No telling what we'll be forced to breathe next." His gaze returned to the forward viewscreen.

An extremely serious chief engineer stared back at him. Scott put a hand over his mouth, coughed hard a couple of times. "I heard, Captain ... I'll get right on that crew."

"The main recreation room, Scotty." He nodded as Kirk switched off.

A small measure of sanity returned to the Bridge as Kirk and Spock strove frantically to discover a path through the labyrinth of contradictions their central computer had created. It wasn't long before M'ress indicated a call for Kirk and he was forced to turn his attention from the harried research back to the main viewscreen.

The image that appeared was Scott, but now the background was different. It showed busy men and women working in an otherwise deserted corridor, instead of in Engineering. He knew where the chief engineer was, now.

"How's that door coming, Scotty?"

Scott's voice was filled with despair, discouragement. "None of our power tools work, Captain! The laser drill, standard metal-cutting saws, drills ... nothin'. Near as I can figure, some kind of internal energy drain is operatin' here.

"I tried them on ship's power first. The big drill didn't even turn over. We got a couple of spins from a battery-powered saw before it died. After that, nothin' so much as burped. Whatever's suckin' this stuff dry is as efficient as it is selective."

The view jerked slightly as he moved aside and readjusted the corridor visual pickup. Now Kirk was able to see exactly how the work was proceeding. Several crew members were attacking the rec room with crowbars while another pounded a steel wedge into the doorway jamb with a sledgehammer.

"As you can see, we're givin' it a mighty go with manual equipment." Scott almost smiled. "We've got some awfully primitive stuff on board, Captain. Whoever wrote out cruiser stores either had a vivid imagination or secret fondness for sweat. Whoever it was, I'm glad he included some old-fashioned persuaders among all the electronics." He chuckled. This time, it didn't hurt.

"Keep at it, Scotty. We've got three people in there whose lives may depend on it." He paused. "I hope the worst that's happened to them is that they've laughed themselves sick."

"We'll have 'em out any minute, sir," Scott assured him, more to boost the Captain's spirits than because it was true. "No need to worry . . ."

McCoy stopped, exhausted. Sulu and Uhura had long since outdistanced him. Now they turned and waited patiently for him to catch up. Sulu waved.

"Come on, Doctor, we must be close to the outside wall by now."

McCoy shook his head, wondering if the echo of his voice would reach them. "You two better go on without me—cold's finally gotten to my legs. We may not even be walking in a straight line. Illusion . . . everything's fake. Maybe . . . maybe you can hit the door by chance . . . if you move fast. You won't, with me." He sat down in the snow. He could no longer feel anything below his ankles.

"Doctor," Uhura began as she and Sulu walked back to him, "we're not going to . . ."

She stopped. The enclosed environment changed. The sensation was similar to the feeling of temporal–physical displacement one felt when transporting.

Gone were the snow, the cold, wind and ice. Instead of clinging white drifts they found themselves standing on a patio of pink marble, surrounded by gleaming Corinthian columns out of an ancient Hellenic frieze. The patio was encircled by a lush green lawn, recently watered. Tall, manicured hedges walled them in. The soothing simulacrum was complete even to the position of the warm sun in the sky, the light breeze scented with date blossoms, even drifting butterflies. The maniac in control of the rec room annex was nothing if not thorough.

"Well, what do you know," Sulu murmured, half-appreciatively. "Come on, Doctor, looks like we're finally going to get out of here."

McCoy was too tired to dispute the helmsman, and he sincerely wanted to agree with him. They waited until he hauled himself up on thawing legs and started toward the one opening visible in the surrounding hedge. He passed them, stopped at the entrance. Sulu and Uhura slowed, aware that something was wrong. When he turned back, his voice reflected a weariness born of pessimistic expectation once more born out.

"I don't mean to discourage you, Sulu, but this may not be as simple as you think."

The helmsman eyed him questioningly. Rather than reply, McCoy beckoned them to come ahead. They came up beside him and looked slightly to the left.

The hedge there was far taller than any of them. It opened into two new pathways. A short sally showed that these in turn branched into several more and broke up again into no one knew how many equally confusing mazes.

Sulu looked disconsolate, while Uhura offered an enlightening combination of Swahili, English, and Simbian curses.

"Ever wonder how the rat feels?" McCoy grinned faintly. "I was afraid something like this might happen." He leaned back against the artificial foliage; it gave like real brush.

"Any time it wants to, the rec room computer can be programmed to decoy us with an infinite arrangement of fake walls and exits. Apparently that's not enough for it. It's gone one step further." He gestured at the first division in the green wall.

"We could wander around in this old-fashioned garden maze until we all grew long wrinkles and blank expressions. One thing you can bet on. The last place any of these pathways lead is *out*."

Sulu tried to find a bright side. "At least we know where we are. We might as well stay here."

"Yes, that's right," agreed Uhura hopefully. "We're probably closer to the corridor wall than we were when we started walking."

"Are you sure?" McCoy asked, staring past her. "Take a look behind you."

The two junior officers turned. Marble columns and patio, green lawn, all were gone now. Stretching away in every direction were duplicates of the featureless hedgerows they now faced. Like it or not, they had been trapped in the maze.

"Where do we go from here?" a discouraged Sulu muttered.

The last thing he expected was an answer. So they were all surprised when it came, shattering both the silence and the hedgerow simulacrum with a violent crash.

A section of brush suddenly collapsed inward toward them, and they had a view into the next dimension. The inside of the rectangular section was green; but the other side was made of metal. It was the corridor they had entered from that showed beyond. Their sense of direction must have been right even through the snow and wind.

No wonder their assailant had been forced to alter their environment . . . they had been too close to finding their way out.

Standing in the rough-edged opening, through which the perfume of standard composition ship-air now poured, were a worried Commander Scott and several engineering techs armed with crowbars, hammers and picks.

Uhura let out a relieved sigh and slumped against Sulu, who staggered. He suddenly was aware that he was more tired than he had believed possible.

McCoy started forward—and then stopped dead, a peculiar expression twisting his features.

"Scotty," he said strangely, "what's behind you?"

Scott looked understandably puzzled. "Behind me?" He hesitated. Dr. McCoy sounded serious, so he looked right then left. "Service corridor leading off east and. west. What in heaven's name . . . ?"

McCoy walked up to him and extended a hand. Scott looked at him, started to say something and then shook it firmly. As he did so a broad smile spread across the doctor's face.

"I know every groove and callus in that palm," he explained with satisfaction. "If you're an illusion, Scotty, you're the best crafted one this rec room ever devised."

"Illusion?" Scott gaped. "By the holy heather, the Captain about worries himself to death over what hap-

pened to you three, I nearly break my own back and
those of this crew here to get you out, and you have
the brass to call me an illusion? McCullhans and
Scotts, I'll show you who's an illusion!"

"Easy, Scotty, easy," McCoy gentled. "I plead recreational fatigue."

The chief engineer's brow wrinkled. "Recreational
. . . what's that?"

"A new disease recently made up especially for the
three of us." He gestured at Sulu and Uhura. "We've
been overentertained for the last few hours." Then he
sat down on the battered-in door and took off his
shoes.

Scott watched him in dumbfoundment until the
socks started to come off, then his eyes widened. "What
happened to your feet?"

"Come on, Scotty, I'm disappointed in you. You
should recognize it—surely you've seen enough cases
to."

It hit Scott seconds later. "Frostbite . . . in the rec
room?" He looked incredulous.

"Seems impossible, doesn't it?"

"No . . . no, as a matter of fact, it doesn't. You don't
have a true picture of what's been goin' on, any of you.
You've been out of touch for the last several hours. I
forgot that, for a minute. No, nothin' that happened to
you in there could surprise me."

"The only thing I'm interested in getting in touch
with now," McCoy countered with verve, "is the idiot
who's responsible."

"I can help you there," Scott informed them. "We
know who the idiot is."

"The culprit's been arrested, then?" McCoy asked.
"I'll be interested to see how far over the edge he actually is."

Scott didn't smile. "He hasn't been arrested, and is
not likely to be—and you'd have a devil of a time
prescribing treatment."

"Tell me about it when I get to the Bridge. First the
three of us have to make a little detour to Sick Bay.
Sulu and Uhura have assorted bruises and strains that

require attention, and I think I have to stick my pods in the cooker for a bit . . ."

He rubbed ruefully at his damaged feet as he fought to make sense of Scott's words . . .

VIII

"There's no need for either of you to stand this shift," Kirk told Sulu and Uhura when they returned to the Bridge. McCoy came along with them.

Both lieutenants ignored him as they relieved Arex and M'ress. "Sorry, Captain, but you'll have to order us out," Sulu objected.

"And as you can see," Uhura added, "we took the precaution of bringing Dr. McCoy along with us—in case we needed an irrefutable medical opinion."

"Seems I'm outnumbered and outflanked," Kirk mumbled, concealing his pleasure at their safe return. "What is your irrefutable medical opinion, Bones?"

"Both of them are fully fit for duty, Jim. You might even say anxious."

"I see. Then I might as well quit pretending and admit how glad I am to see you both back on the Bridge. We had some anxious moments trying to figure out what our berserk computer was doing to you all."

"Not as anxious as we did," McCoy confirmed. "You know what we went through by now—you did see my preliminary report?"

"I saw what you dictated to the medical records log, if that's what you mean," Kirk replied unenthusiastically. "I'd prefer a less technical description."

"Sure . . . if you'll grant me one request."

"Anything within reason and regulations, Bones."

McCoy crossed his arms and rubbed both biceps. "Could you turn up the heat on the Bridge? I *know* it's my imagination, but I haven't felt really comfortable since we left that madhouse."

120

Kirk chuckled, then self-consciously cut it off. He had already done more than enough laughing for one day.

"As to your description," McCoy began, only to have Spock interrupt him.

"Captain, we're getting under way ... the main drive has been activated."

"Uhura, on the double, get me Chief Scott."

"Yes, sir." A pause, then a slightly surprised reply. "Sir, Mr. Scott just called in, trying to get in touch with *you*. He reports that despite the fact every sensor and gauge reads negative action, the warp drive *is* operating. He has already tried every emergency procedure ... even attempted to shut down the control reactors. Nothing works."

"I heard that the central computer's been responsible for all the trouble," McCoy said. "What's it up to now?"

"Sir, the helm no longer responds," a troubled Sulu reported. "We're coming about to a new heading."

"Very well, Lieutenant," a resigned Kirk said. "As soon as our course stabilizes, give me a full plotting."

There was silence for several minutes as Sulu studied his readouts, then reported, "Course stabilizing, sir ... three-seven-two mark twelve."

Kirk did some quick mental calculation. Roughly translated, those figures meant they were heading back toward the neutral zone, back toward three waiting Romulan cruisers.

"And you can bet they'll be gunning for us, after the way we slipped by them," Kirk said minutes later.

A high, hysterical and by now all-too-familiar chirping echoed through the bridge. It sounded for all the world like a crazed electric cuckoo loose in its clock— and the analogy was not so far wrong.

"Speed increasing, sir," Sulu informed him. "We'll round the energy field any minute—sensors are picking up three vessels." He worked controls. "Long-range scanners show them to be Romulan warships."

"Now *that's* a surprise," Kirk muttered.

"Decelerating, sir," the helmsman continued. Kirk's chair intercom buzzed.

"Bridge, Captain speaking."

"Scott, Captain." The chief engineer sounded concerned. "I've no idea what it means, but I'm receivin' information that the ship's inorganic metallic fabrication facilities have been workin' overtime ever since we started up again."

"Any indication what the computer's up to, Mr. Scott?"

"I kinna tell, sir, that whole deck section's been sealed off."

"Captain . . ."

"Just a minute, Uhura." He turned back to the mike. "Let me know if you find anything out, Scotty."

"Aye, sir, Engineering out."

"What is it, Uhura?"

"Sir, monitors indicate the main cargo hatch is opening. I'll swing the rear scanners on it."

"Yes . . . do so, Lieutenant," he agreed absently. His thoughts were running into each other, threads of one frantic solution meshing with the wrong problem. Slow down, he wanted to shout! Slow down—things were happening too fast. As soon as he thought he was getting one problem under control, something new cropped up to shove it aside.

The rear of the ship appeared on the viewscreen as Uhura manipulated the scanners mounted on the stern. She worked controls and the field of view rotated. Something white and glowing slid past.

"Bring that back, Lieutenant," Kirk ordered hurriedly. Slowly the scanner retraced its path, until it was focused on the rear cargo hatch. Two massive clamshell doors were separating. The spot of brightness was the cargo hold itself, brightly lit from within.

Something was occluding that brightness . . . something gigantic.

A huge, highly reflective mass of constantly changing shape billowed from the open hatch. Light from the starship's running lights and the surrounding stars gleamed in that expanding metal skin. It drifted behind the *Enterprise,* still growing rapidly, as the cargo doors closed.

"Keep your scanners on that, Lieutenant—Mr. Sulu, you stay with the Romulans."

Acknowledgment was prompt from both consoles. "What in heaven's name is going on now?" McCoy wondered.

"Your guess is probably better than mine, Bones," Kirk confessed. "You've experienced the computer's whimsy longer than anyone."

"Maybe . . . but I never saw anything like *that* before."

They stared in rapt fascination at the image conveyed by the scanners. It became apparent that the monstrous shape was steadily inflating.

"It looks like some kind of metal balloon, Jim. But what on Earth's it for?"

"If the cargo doors open again and a gigantic pin starts to come out, we'll know," ventured Sulu. "It'd be in keeping with the computer's actions so far."

"I fail to see the connection, Mr. Sulu," a curious Spock observed."

"Sulu's supposition is wrong, anyway, Spock," Kirk told him. "There wouldn't be any noise."

Spock did not appear enlightened. "Noise? Captain, I confess I am puzzled by . . ." He stopped abruptly, peering hard into his own viewer.

"What is it, Spock?"

"Odd . . . the inflatable object is acquiring an outline which superficially resembles a ship."

"I see it now," Sulu agreed excitedly. "It looks like one of the old Federation dreadnoughts—the class that was never built because all that weaponry was never needed."

"Whatever it is, it's about twenty times our size," noted Kirk.

"Captain, we're changing course again," Sulu said. "We're pulling away from it slightly."

"What have the Romulans been doing? We've been within range of their scanners for several minutes now."

"I believe they started toward us several minutes ago, Captain," Spock declared, checking readouts, "but their subsequent movements have been erratic. They have presently terminated all signs of approach. Undoubtedly the sudden appearance of a warship twenty times their size has occasioned some hasty discussion among the Romulan command."

"I'll bet," Kirk agreed, smiling despite his own ignorance of what the computer was up to.

McCoy was less amused. "It may look like a dreadnought now, but if they approach within visual pickup range they'll obtain a detailed fix on it and see that it's nothing more than inflated foil—and they won't think it funny."

"For the present, though, you must admit that the Romulans *have* halted."

"So it's an effective bluff—I see that, Spock. But it won't last long. It'll only infuriate them more." He shrugged. "More cybernetic madness."

"Unless there's a message in it," Kirk whispered thoughtfully.

Spock's brows contracted. "If you would elaborate, Captain."

"Yes, Jim," McCoy wondered, eyeing him steadily, "who's madness are you talking about?" He eyed Kirk in such a way as to indicate that perhaps the central computer wasn't the only brain on board that had gone a little dotty.

"Bones, sometimes to understand madness you have to think like a madman—no, don't be alarmed," Kirk added at the look that suddenly appeared on the good doctor's face. "I mean that this is a time to look for the inner logic.

"All that's happening is that the *Enterprise* is pulling her biggest practical joke so far—only this time it's on the Romulans."

"Are you suggesting," Spock asked, "that the *Enterprise* is capable of experiencing a desire for revenge?"

"What else? She's going to make fools of them by inducing them to attack a balloon, and the Romulans fear disgrace even more than death."

"It is still not possible, Captain. Revenge is a purely emotional action."

"What would you think of a Vulcan who displayed a desire for revenge, Spock?"

"Why, we would try to cure him of his madn—I see, Captain. Your point is well taken. And I confess I have no alternative explanation for the computer's present actions." His gaze returned to the sensor image of the drifting cruisers.

"However, I am most interested just now in the effect of the ploy and not in the motivation behind it . . ."

The alien triumvirate of destruction hovered well outside combat range and considered the colossal apparition that had appeared alongside their target.

On board the heavy cruiser which formed the vanguard of the Romulan task force, an impatient Commander scratched his arm and studied the gargantuan image, trying to imagine how the Federation had concealed a warship of such size from Imperial spies. It didn't seem possible . . . yet there it was.

As soon as it had appeared, the *Enterprise* had started off on a new course back toward Federation territory—but slowly, almost challengingly. It was almost as if Kirk were daring him to pursue, trying to lure him into attacking.

He would have to make a decision soon, or their intended prey would make good its escape. To have failed the Plan once was bad enough. To have the quarry return to tweak the Imperial nose and saunter off at cruising speed was infuriating.

One drawback to renewed pursuit, however, was the apparent indifference with which this new vessel squatted in midspace and regarded the Imperial force. It showed no inclination either to attack or retreat. Despite its size, he felt certain his three smaller vessels could outmaneuver it.

Outgunning it was another matter entirely.

"No response to our calls, Commander," his communications officer reported.

"They have refused surrender. Very well. Large it may be, but foolish is its commander. We will not permit so great a prize to escape." He called to his helmsman. "Notify the others—we will attack according to the fourth helical scheme."

"Yes, Commander!"

The order was passed. Weaving in and about several common points designated by their battle computers, the three Romulan cruisers advanced at assault speed. At extreme range they opened fire in a carefully integrated sequence. Photon bombs which had already proven so effective against the *Enterprise* were flung ahead in a complex half-predetermined, half-random pattern that no ship's defenses could avoid.

The object of this triple barrage did not. Several of the powerful explosives struck the anodized skin and blew gaping holes in the false mass. With no outside pressure to collapse it, the bloated construct of micron-thick foil held its shape. Held it firmly enough for the gaping wounds to show that it was completely hollow inside.

As he ingested this unexpected development, the Romulan commander's eyes grew almost as large as the cavernous gaps his expensive explosives had ripped in the thin metal.

"Fooled . . . tricked . . . insult, insult!" he howled, apoplectic with anger. "Gravest offense . . . most heinous perversion of martial chivalry. Contact . . . contact the *Enterprise!*" he sputtered at his communications officer.

That worthy hurried to comply. "We have made contact, sir," he reported seconds later.

"Put them through."

The link was cleared—and immediately a high, wavering sound washed over the Romulan bridge. One did not have to be a specialist in Federation emotional utterances to recognize it as laughter.

Of course, the Romulan commander had no knowledge of its true source . . . but it was enough for him to know that it came from the *Enterprise*.

All pretense at caution vanished under that teasing giggle.

"Full pursuit speed!" he roared. "I want that ship reduced to dust, to particles, to its component elements."

"Honored Commander," the helmsman protested timidly, "they have some distance on us, and they are no longer within the neutral zone."

Laughter continued to roll across the Romulan Bridge. "Extinguish that! And pursue!"

On board another Bridge the same laughter still echoed, though it was beginning to subside. "Captain," Sulu noted, "the Romulans are giving chase."

McCoy let out a long whistle. "They must be a little crazed themselves to follow us this deep into Federation territory, now that they can't surprise us like they did before."

"I don't care about that. I don't even care about the Romulans," Kirk cried. McCoy's expression narrowed. There was an alien, uncharacteristic fearfulness in the captain's voice. "I just want to avoid that energy field.

"Helmsman, do you have a fix on its present position? For nova's sake, stay away from there!"

Everyone had spun to stare in disbelief at Kirk, who sat all but trembling in the command chair, slumped low into the seat.

It looked to Sulu as if the captain were shivering like a man frightened half to death. In fact, this sudden transformation of the indomitable captain into a seeming basket case was so startling everyone was struck speechless.

"I have it plotted, sir," Sulu was finally able to reply ... since some sort of reassurance seemed to be necessary. "Our present course takes us nowhere near it."

The relief in Kirk's shaken countenance was almost palpable. "Thank God," he muttered shakily, "I couldn't face that traverse again."

"Sir, if I may be permitted," Sulu continued, unable to keep the tinge of chastisement clear of his tone, "the damage we incurred during the actual passage was mini . . ."

A traitorous feminine voice cut him off. "Why should the thought of making another passage scare you . . . there is no reason for it. I sustained only minimal damage in making the actual passage."

"It's not that . . . not that," Kirk replied in evident terror. "It's the idea of having your body, every cell and nerve, lanced through and through with radiation we know nothing about . . . the thought of what that

might do to one's internal make-up ..." He actually
shuddered. "The thought petrifies me."

"How very interesting," the voice murmured sweetly.
The whine of gyros sounded.

"Sir ..." Sulu worked uselessly at his instrumentation. "We're changing course again. The energy field
lies on the periphery of our long-range sensors, but we
seem to be heading straight for it ... again."

"No!" Kirk was shaking so hard he could barely
lean forward. "We can't be ... not again."

Laughter reverberated around them ... laughter
that was neither human nor sane.

"Reverse direction, Mr. Sulu!"

The helmsman made a futile effort to provoke some
response from his console, then looked back and
shrugged helplessly. "I can't, sir. Controls are still
frozen. Sir, if I may say, we've nothing to worry about
so. We know ..."

"I can't take that again," Kirk babbled, "I can't take
that again ..."

The view ahead began to shine as the first effects of
the radiant cloud made themselves felt. Barely percep-
tibly at first, then unmistakably, the deck commenced
to oscillate underfoot. Vibration intensified until it was
just shy of being severe.

Now the scanners stepped down the overpowering
panoply of color to where it was bearable by human
eyes.

Kirk remained cowering in the command chair, his
hands clutching tightly to the arms. Appropriate
discussion would have continued about the captain's
startling collapse of nerve, only there was plenty to do
at the moment to insure that the *Enterprise* held together during its passage through the field.

There was no *real* reason for concern. After all, they
had made this difficult passage once before. Presumably they would do it again. But this time, it would be
better to remain intent at one's job, welded to one's instruments—what with the central computer out of control and the captain apparently paralyzed by fear.

Plenty of time for Dr. McCoy to treat the commander once the ship was safely through ...

So, while the matter never strayed completely from their minds, everyone remained glued to his post and ignored the quivering figure which shook in the command chair—ignored also the ripples of mirth that steadily issued from the Bridge speakers.

Another set of vibrations commenced not far behind them, as the maddened Romulans—their caution overcome by fury—entered the energy cloud in engine-straining pursuit.

The *Enterprise*'s abrupt course change, which had brought it swooping around within near firing range, was puzzling and unreasonable enough to puncture the Romulan commander's suit of anger. Already deep within Federation territory and with a clear lead, what profit could the *Enterprise*'s commander see in a swing back toward the neutral zone and his pursuers?

It unnerved him more than he cared to admit. One thing the Romulans had learned not to despise in their dealings with the Federation was the fiendish subtlety of high-ranking humans like Kirk.

So he consulted with his officers and with the commanders of his other ships. They dumped their worries into their computers and frantically hunted for a rationale behind the inexplicable maneuver. The cybernetic shrugs that resulted did little to alleviate their concern . . .

The Romulan helmsman held tightly to one arm of his chair while his other fluttered helplessly over his abruptly unresponsive console. Assured of its new ineffectualness, he turned and caught the eye of his already brooding commander.

"Sir, our sensors are useless while in this field. We've lost all contact with the Federation ship."

That was the final *ubuz* as far as the commander was concerned. "First the *Enterprise* alters a heading on which it had a fair chance of escaping or of contacting help, in order to return within range of a superior force. Then it draws us into this mysterious field. Now it appears they cannot be located." What unknown weaponry, what new insult might Kirk be preparing to unleash on them?

The combination of uncertainties was too much for

the already jittery commander. His ship was being subjected to a battering which was strong, but not dangerous, as yet. The operative word was "yet." It offered a
chance—maybe the last chance—to withdraw with
some shred of honor.

Also, his liver was bothering him.

"We must clear this field before our ships break up.
Bring us about on a new heading, navigator, for
home."

"You're going to let them get away, sir? After the
way they've taunted us, insulted us?"

"If we can no longer locate them," the commander
replied dryly, not wishing to fight with his own officers,
"that strikes me as a reasonable evaluation of our
present circumstances. I suggest attending to your duties, Varpa. These require you to obey orders ... no
more. Do so."

Varpa started to say more, suddenly became aware a
proximity mine field was an inauspicious place to dance
a polka, and shut up.

Pleased by the silence, the commander began to
compose his report to Fleet Headquarters: Surreptitious
Operations Bureau. As he did so, he regarded the fore
viewscreen, which offered a picture of the scintillating,
radiant energy field ... now shrinking rapidly behind
them.

Hopefully, somewhere within its magnificently colored distortion of space and matter, the thrice-cursed
Enterprise was already tearing itself to pieces ...

The *Enterprise*, however, was holding together very
nicely, thank you. So far it had resisted the corrosive
efforts of both the radiation and the Romulan invec-
tive.

More concern was felt over the coherence, or lack
thereof, of its captain. But his terror seemed to fade
slightly when an awkward fluttering cracked the steady
laughter still issuing from the speakers.

He began to look normal again when the unsteady
chuckling started to waver noticeably.

"Tricked," the computer voice abruptly claimed.
"Not fair ... not fair ..." Laughter and peevish over-
tone were beginning to fade rapidly now.

"What the . . . what's happening to it?" McCoy queried, holding tightly for support to the back of the command chair.

The final giggle sounded . . . an unintelligent, choking cough. Then all was quiet.

When Kirk spoke again, it was immediately clear that his *fear* had vanished along with the laughter. "Bones, the worst thing you can do to a practical joker is to play a practical joke on him." His tone was grim but no longer anxious. "Although this is one joke whose successful outcome had something more than a laugh riding on it."

"We're clear of the field, sir," Sulu informed him.

"Good. Change course two degrees up. Same heading. Resume standard cruising speed."

The helmsman looked doubtful, but proceeded to try and comply. His expression and voice brightened the moment he touched the first controls. "All instrumentation is responding normally now, Captain. No indication of any interference with helm functions. Engine response is normal, too."

"And I am receiving standard response in all computer modes," Spock declared. "Higher logic and intuitive reasoning functions check out normal . . . with no intimation of a desire to operate on their own." He glanced approvingly across at Kirk.

"That last pass through the energy field apparently reversed the damaging effects of our initial incursion."

"So that's why you were so vocal in your *horror* of another ride through," McCoy exclaimed as understanding dawned. "And all the time you had us thinking you'd slipped your helm."

"Something radical *had* to be tried, Bones. Frankly, when it first occurred to me, I didn't think the idea made much sense . . . which made it seem perfectly appropriate, in light of the way the computer was acting."

"A well-conceived and efficiently executed deception, Captain," complimented his first officer.

Kirk grinned wanly. "Not entirely deception, Mr. Spock. I *was* frightened . . . not of another passage through the field, but of what the computer might try next. Its sense of humor was becoming increasingly sadistic."

"Amen to that!" McCoy commented fervently.

"What I had to do," Kirk continued, leaning back in the command chair, "was redirect the anxiety I was feeling and let it run away with me."

"You are too modest, Captain," Spock commented. "You had everyone fooled—all of us, besides the computer. I could never have carried off the same masquerade myself."

"Needless to say," needled McCoy.

Spock ignored him.

"The effects of the field on our computer circuitry and operation have been thoroughly documented by independent means," Spock continued, studying his library console. "They will provide much material for dissection by Federation cybernetics experts. I envision many hours of investigative perusal myself."

"Hold it," Uhura suddenly exclaimed. "Captain, I'm picking up Romulan intership and intercom transmissions—evidently something's gone wrong with their broadcast equipment."

Kirk looked puzzled. "More than *wrong,* Lieutenant. Aside from the waste of power, putting intercom transmissions on ship-to-ship frequencies is a serious breach of comm security. I wonder what—Uhura, what are you smiling at?"

"I'll put it on the Bridge speakers, sir." She adjusted controls.

The first voice they heard happened to be that of the task force commander railing at his engineering staff.

". . . and turn off those food synthesizers!" he was shouting as the broadcast cleared. "We're knee-deep in hot fudge sundaes, and they're starting to impede passage in the corridors!"

The arguments from all three ships and numerous sections went on in that vein—increasingly confused, increasingly angry, increasingly frustrated.

McCoy grinned broadly. "I didn't even know the Romulans knew what a hot fudge sundae was—much less that their fabricators were capable of synthesizing one."

"I daresay that the entire situation is rather upsetting to them," Kirk chuckled. "It would seem that something's gone wrong with their computers."

"Shall we tell them how they can reverse the effects of the field, Jim?"

"Oh, eventually, I suppose. After all, I don't think I'd want even the Romulans to go through too much of what we've been subjected to. But ... let's not spoil their fun just yet."

The laughter that sounded on the Bridge then was spontaneous—and decidedly non-mechanical in origin. To Spock, however, it was all the same, even if the motivation behind it was less threatening.

"Inexplicable, incomprehensible and irrational," he muttered, turning back to his console. He set about resuming his theoretical studies where he had been forced to leave off when the Romulans had attacked. Laughter filled the air around him.

There was one important difference, though. This non-gaseous stimulation didn't give him a headache.

And while he mused on his research and his companions made jokes about the Romulans' present predicament, he couldn't know that events had been set in motion which would prove of greater importance than anything examination of the records of the central computer's temporary hysteria could produce ...

PART III

HOW SHARPER THAN A
SERPENT'S TOOTH

(Adapted from a script by Russell Bates and David Wise)

IX

The network of detector drones and interwoven patrols which guarded the Federation home worlds, its industrial and population centers, was as thorough and as efficient as that highly advanced multiracial civilization could make it. It was designed to protect and defend against even a surprise Klingon attack in force.

A single ship, moving at high speed and employing radical evasive maneuvers, could conceivably penetrate that electronic web. The one which did so moved in a predictable, straight path and made no attempt to disguise its destination. It compensated for the lack of concealment by moving at a speed previously thought impossible.

No one could be sure, but the probe executed such extreme changes of direction at such incredible velocities that it seemed certain it was uninhabited. Also, it went about its business with supreme indifference to all attempts at contact. When all such methods were exhausted, and the probe continued to refuse repeated warnings to steer clear of Federation worlds, the Federation council reluctantly decided to destroy the interloper. This decision was modified by the science councilor to include some initial attempt to capture the craft. The Federation engineering division desired at least a look at those remarkable engines.

The attempt at capture met with the same result as those at destruction, however. No Federation warship could overtake it, and the alien interloper did not linger in the vicinity of any armed vessel it approached. So in spite of intensive efforts to halt it, the probe performed the most rapid survey of the United Federation Systems in history ... and it did so with a silence that was an unnerving as it was baffling.

All the while, however, the Federation's most advanced electronic predictors were slowly analyzing the drone's performance. Continued observation showed that it held to a prescribed pattern of survey and dodge, inspection and flight.

At each new world, larger and stronger Federation forces closed in on the craft. Each was programmed with a particular attack pattern, which was backed by a third set of reinforcements that would stand by in case the probe escaped the first two. Soon entire fleets had been mobilized in a mounting attempt to corner a single, uninhabited, as yet inoffensive ship.

The problem was that the probe never lingered long enough for the huge forces to catch up with it. Nonetheless, the Vulcan logicians programming the predictors were certain that given enough time, they would trap the drone in a maze of phasers and torpedoes so intense that nothing could escape. But they weren't given the required time. The probe executed its final survey—a brief, yet impressively thorough multiple circuit of Earth itself.

Even as the most powerful Federation force so far was weaving its way toward the probe, it paused in free space and aligned itself toward a predetermined point. It appeared to be blithely unconcerned with the increasing possibility of annihilation. Once positioned, the probe discharged an extremely high-frequency, lengthy blast of energy. The thunderous broadcast utilized far more power than it seemed a ship of that modest size could muster.

The broadcast lasted only a few minutes. At its conclusion, the probe activated its engines. It disintegrated just outside the orbit of Luna in an explosion of sobering magnitude. Auroras formed as far south as Hong Kong and Istanbul for several weeks, and most of the transmitting equipment on Earth's lone satellite required extensive repair immediately thereafter.

The mysterious intruder was gone. Several fragments of eyelash-size metal gave no clue to its origin. It had carried out its lengthy mission for the incomprehensible motives of as yet unknown beings.

From where had it come? Who had constructed such a marvelous machine and what were their intentions? Why had it shunned all contact with Federation intelligences? These obvious questions and more were asked again and again by important individuals serving in the highest echelons of Federation government. And those whom they asked for the answers could only shrug.

A measure of the importance attached to the enigmatic visitation was the readiness with which the Klingons and Romulans cooperated. The wonder at this vanished when both opponents of the Federation sheepishly admitted that before the Federation had been surveyed, their own respective empires had been similarly inspected. Though no one could be certain, it appeared that the same isolated probe had been involved in each instance.

A few zealots within the government warned that it might all be an elaborate plot, concocted by the Klingons and/or Romulans to obtain military information from frightened government authorities.

Impartial engineering experts quashed such thoughts immediately . . . neither Klingon or adaptive Romulan physics were even close to producing something as advanced as their visitor had been. If they were, it was ruthlessly pointed out, they would be putting it to more effective use than casual surveillance.

The intricate recording equipment based on Luna, on Earth and on Titan could track even the path of a butterfly at interstellar distances. So when the suicidal probe began regurgitating its concentrated information, those several stations were already tracking it. They detected the transmission the instant it began, recorded it minutely for rechecking at later leisure.

So efficient was that tracking equipment, however, that no rechecks were required, no computer enhancement of that blindingly powerful signal necessary. Instantaneous triangulation was produced by the three stations.

The beam had erupted from the probe along a line as clear and precise as white ink on a blackboard.

It was along that path that the *Enterprise* had been ordered to proceed.

The amount of energy expended in that minutes-long broadcast had been immense—far in excess of anything Federation science was capable of. And although that energy was still on the near side of infinite, there was reason enough to believe that the receiving end of the transmission might lie outside this galaxy ...

If that were the case, Kirk thought to himself, the *Enterprise* could have rather a longer trip than anyone expected. No one had anticipated what the orders might be if she found herself poised on the rim of such extremes.

But Kirk had to consider that the beam had intercepted no known star systems, not even suns without planets, and they were now well outside Federation boundaries. He idly watched Spock at work with the library computer and sighed. They had been retracing the course Starfleet had supplied for weeks now.

No telling how long this could go on. The orders had been for the *Enterprise* to proceed until, as the ethereally worded document stated: "all possible doubt has been removed as to the potential dangers posed to the Federated peoples by the alien intruder."

That order was sufficiently vague to keep them cruising for months, even years, unless recalled—or until the halfway point of their irreplaceable supplies was reached.

Lately Kirk had been subject to a particularly chilling nightmare. Some junior clerk at Starfleet headquarters was continually misplacing the *Enterprise* file, or allowing the recall orders to slip down behind some spool storage case, or accidentally erasing all record of the cruiser from the Starfleet central computer.

The ship was forgotten. It continued on, taking on new stores at various puzzled worlds, whose inhabitants stared sadly at the wrinkled, white-haired crew trapped in its Tantalus-like quest.

He grew aware of a presence next to him. The presence was clearing its throat delicately. "What ...? Oh ..."

Turning away from the patient yeoman, Kirk studied the order form the latter had handed to him. Hmmm . . . standard request for use of the main recreation room.

For a second he almost handed it back unsigned, remembering what had nearly happened to McCoy, Sulu and Uhura in that same room several weeks ago. But the story of their entrapment in that chamber had circulated throughout the ship. A scare like that would die hard. He doubted anyone would go in for any exotic manipulations of the environment for a while. It was one thing to be threatened on a new, alien world— quite another when your own games facilities turned on you.

Someone wanted the proper atmosphere for a birth-day party of some such, no doubt. He signed the chit, saluted casually as the yeoman departed, and turned his gaze to the view forward.

The screen displayed the same gloriously monot-onous image it had for days and days—unfamiliar star patterns speckling the blackness. Kirk found himself growing sick of unfamiliar star patterns speckling the blackness. If they didn't encounter something soon—a derelict spacecraft, a postal drop, anything—he was going to have Uhura tight-beam the nearest starbase and patch him through to fleet headquarters, where he could give vent to his emotions.

He began running his speech over in his head. He would discourse on the futility of the entire expedition and add some appropriate thoughts about the power wielded by a few panicked bureaucrats. Above all, this expedition was proving to be a sinful waste of ship's power and crewpower.

He forced himself to clear the welling irritation from his voice as he called for the current status report from his first officer.

Spock paused an instant at the gooseneck viewer, checked another sensor before turning to face Kirk. "We are continuing along the path plotted by Starfleet Central, Captain. However, I feel it is time for me to point out that the accuracy of that plotting diffuses with every parsec we cover.

"It has now reached the point where . . . ," he hesitated long enough to check a last readout, ". . . the margin of divergence has increased to nearly a tenth of a degree."

Kirk nodded. "I see. Not a serious range of error . . . if we're hunting for a planet. But if we're looking for a ship, we could miss it by many trillions of kilometers. Soon that'll be true for a star system, too.

"What would you recommend, Mr. Spock?"

"Reducing our speed to accommodate our long-range, peripheral sensing equipment, so that we do not rush past anything such as a small vessel."

"Reasonable—though I don't like the idea of cutting our speed. Mr. Walking Bear, bring us down to warp-factor two."

The ensign who was occupying Sulu's position usually drew the third shift—when both Kirk and Spock were off-duty and asleep. Sulu, however, had elected to take some extra time off that he had accumulated, and Walking Bear had gladly volunteered for the opportunity to serve with the ship's executive command.

He had performed well so far, Kirk mused. Must remember to make note of the ensign's competence in the supplementary log. Unaware that he was being subjected to close scrutiny, Walking Bear made the necessary adjustments. "Aye, sir, warp-factor two."

His accent was faint, but the long black hair and rich rust color marked him as an Amerind of the North American Southwest. Kirk struggled to recall an early academy seminar in Basic Ethnics.

It was impossible to be more than cursorily familiar with the background of every one of the *Enterprise*'s four hundred thirty assigned personnel. That didn't stop the captain from trying, however. It was something with a hard *ch* sound in it, now . . .

Kirk wondered how much time the ensign had in . . . perhaps he was eligible for promotion to lieutenant. Even though this expedition had proven routine, maybe he could come up with some way to test the young helmsman's mettle.

As it developed, he would be spared the trouble . . .

"Captain," Arex reported, "sensors have picked up a vessel at extreme range."

"Any indication as to heading, Mr. Arex?"

The navigation officer studied his readouts a moment longer, made a high, snuffling sound as he expelled air through high-ridged nostrils.

"It appears to be proceeding on the same plot followed by the alien probe's final broadcast, sir—but the vessel is moving toward us, instead of outward. Approximate speed, warp-three."

"Mr. Spock?"

"Range is still too extreme to attempt detailed observation, Captain." He studied his small viewers. "Possibly this is a second probe. It may be that the first did not complete its assigned task, and merely malfunctioned instead of self-destructing. This may be another drone coming to conclude the operation."

Kirk frowned. "True, Mr. Spock, or it could be the original probe's owner."

"If this one's coming in search of its predecessor, it's not going to find much," Uhura noted.

"Order all stations, yellow alert, Lieutenant," Kirk ordered. "Open standard hailing frequencies." He gestured at the main viewscreen. Despite maximum magnification, the scanners still showed only awesome darkness, strange suns and feathery nebulae.

Whatever it was, maybe it would prove a little more talkative than its super-fast ancestor—if indeed the two craft possessed any relationship at all. They might merely be racing to meet another deep-space explorer like themselves.

The alarm blared throughout the *Enterprise,* sending a second shift scurrying to join the one already on duty.

Kirk stared expectantly at the screen. "Any identification yet, Mr. Spock?" There was no point in straining his eyes, but every Starfleet officer with any real experience was innately certain that his vision could range just a few kilometers further than his ship's electronic scanners. Kirk was no different.

"Not possible yet, Captain," Spock finally declared, "but preliminary sensor analysis indicates an object at least twice our size. Variance could be substantial on closer inspection."

"Not another double of the probe, then," Kirk commented thoughtfully. "I'd feel better if you'd said it was half our size, with variance either way."

"We have no reason to assume it has a hostile intent, Captain," the first officer felt compelled to point out. "If it acts as its possible predecessor did, we can expect it to regard us with studied indifference."

"People who send drone probes through other people's homes without acknowledging even a hello or how-d'you-do don't strike me as overly friendly, either, Spock."

"The one does not imply the other," Spock argued amiably. Discussion was interrupted by the arrival of new information on his instruments. "Regardless, it appears extremely unorthodox in design—much more so than the drone." He made a quick check of the proper records.

"No record of anything like it in the Jane's—and Starfleet information insists there should be no vessels of any known civilization cruising in this extreme region."

"Reduce speed to warp-one, Mr. Walking Bear," Kirk murmured.

"Warp-one, sir?" The ensign looked uncertainly over at Arex. The navigator asked the question spinning through the less-experienced officer's mind.

"Same course, sir?"

"Same course, Mr. Arex. Activate minimal field, ultra-extreme scanner, please." Abruptly the starfield ahead seemed to leap toward them, then come to an abrupt stop. Essentially it remained unchanged. Only now an object lay in its approximate center. It was still only a vague blob of light, but it grew larger with perceptible speed.

"Anything out of those hailing frequencies, Lieutenant?" he asked over his shoulder.

"No response, sir," she told him. "So far it's the probe all over again."

"Continue hailing. Try every frequency you know ... and when you've exhausted those used by the Federation, go through the special Klingon, Romulan, and lesser alliance levels."

"You believe the probe and this vessel may be the work of some small, isolated race, Captain?" Arex wondered.

"Not one we know of, Mr. Arex," Kirk said absently, still staring at the unresolved luminescent image growing larger with the minutes. "But it's possible that whoever is behind both craft has had contact with a smaller independent system like Michaya or the Yoolian worlds. If that's the case, they might respond to such an infrequently used hailing frequency while ignoring ours.

"That doesn't speak well for the supposed friendliness of some of our nominal allies, of course."

"Whatever its purpose or origin, Captain," Spock suddenly announced, staring intently into his gooseneck viewer as he manipulated controls, "it possesses an immense energy aura. The ship itself appears completely encased in it.

"Something on board this craft is generating an enormous quantity of extraneous radiation—for what reason, I cannot tell." More adjustments, new readings—and a new conclusion.

"Fascinating. Additional analysis indicates that the ship's hull is composed wholly of some unknown, unique variety of crystallized ceramic. It appears to possess some characteristics of the lighter metals such as lithium and beryllium while retaining the more malleable properties of—"

Spock's engrossed litany was shattered as a giant, invisible hand clutched the Bridge and shook it violently. Along with everyone else, the first officer concentrated on grabbing for the nearest solid support.

The shaking was accompanied by a loud rumbling. It wasn't a simple, steady vibration; but instead shook them with a distinct up and down, back and forth motion—unlike the effects of the energy field they had traveled through weeks ago while foiling the Romulans' attack.

As the shaking continued, a new sound became audible—a distant declining whine. Kirk recognized the

symptoms of engine shutdown even as Walking Bear
called out, "We're losing speed, sir—and the helm does-
n't answer."

"Dropping to sublight velocity," Arex reported.

Confirmation of his worst suspicions now fulfilled by
the instrumentation, Kirk fought to keep from being
thrown from his seat as he hit the necessary switch.
The rumbling noise was fading, but the shaking continued as violent as ever.

"Bridge to Engineering—Mr. Scott, we're losing
speed. Why?"

An uncharacteristic lag in response followed, though
the reason was understandable. Scott and his subordi-
nates in Engineering were as interested in keeping their
balance as was everyone else.

The chief engineer reported in soon after. "Scott
here. Captain, all our engines are still set for warp-two
thrust . . . but we seem to have run into something like
a wall of solid alloy!"

So his supposition was wrong—the engines weren't
shut down.

"Maximum thrust, Mr. Scott."

"Aye, sir." A pause, then, "I've got 'er wide open,
Captain. We're just not movin'. I dinna know how long
the engine bracings can take the strain before they start
tearin' themselves loose."

"Understood, Scotty. Nice try." He switched off, re-
directing his attention forward. "All engines stop, Mr.
Walking Bear."

The helmsman activated instrumentation before him
that he never expected to be called to activate. Despite
the newness of the operation, his hands moved
smoothly in compliance. As the great warp-drive engines ceased forward thrust, the last vestiges of the
rumbling noise faded away. The shaking ceased with
appalling abruptness.

"All engines stopped, sir," Walking Bear declared
into the unnatural silence on the Bridge.

Kirk tried to moderate their present predicament by
repeating the Words over and over in his head. He
found they provided no more succor than ever. Perhaps he was simply too hyper mentally for artificially

imposed constraints like meditation ever to slow him down. Consequently, he was back on the intercom in a minute, as worried and theory-ridden as ever.

"I want a full damage report as soon as possible, Scotty."

"I'm workin' on it now, Captain," the filtered voice replied. "Everythin' seems minor, so far. No structural damage to the support pylons or braces, and no over-heatin' ... at least, nothing the emergency backups couldn't handle.

"Another couple of minutes of that strain, though ... I think we shut down just in time, sir."

"Thank you, Scotty. Maintain full environmental and defensive power, and effect whatever repairs are required with a minimum of delay."

"Will do, sir. Engineerin' out ..."

Another call, another problem area. "Bridge to Sick Bay ... casualty report."

"McCoy here," came the slightly irritated reply. "No serious injuries, Jim, just the usual lumps and bruises." He managed to make it sound as if the Bridge personnel were personally responsible for the suffering he had to treat.

"What the devil's going on up there? Who's driving ... no, I've got it. Spock decided to see what would happen if everyone on board suddenly jumped up and down in time to a cycling of the artificial gravity."

"I wish that was all it was, Bones. Bridge out." Kirk glanced across at Spock and saw that the first officer appeared not to have heard McCoy's abrasive sally. To ignore an argumentative invitation by McCoy was a sign that his first officer was worried—and when Spock was worried, that was a good time for anyone in the vicinity to make sure their service insurance was fully paid up.

"What are our chances of getting around this obstacle, Spock?"

"I am sorry to say, Captain, that I do not think that is possible. There is no obstacle to go around ... the obstacle is all around *us*. So we cannot retreat, either."

"Its nature?"

"A globular force-field of unknown origin, in which we are presently entrapped. It is obvious that there can be only one source of so strong and sudden an energy projection—the approaching alien ship."

"But we hit the field at warp-two," Walking Bear blurted in confusion, "and practically stopped dead. We should have been pulverized on impact!"

Spock shook his head patiently, touched a lever. The view ahead changed as short-range scanners cut in. The much wider field of view showed a faint, bluish-white glow which the long-range scanner had pierced. It was very much, Kirk mused, like what the interior of a soap bubble might look like.

Spock was lecturing. "We did not hit a stone wall, Mr. Walking Bear. The globular field did not form instantly around us, at a single position in space. It materialized slowly. As it slowed, we slowed against it in proportion. Even so, according to Chief Scott's report, the stress was almost seriously damaging.

"But I confess I do not understand why we did not suffer more than we did. I cannot explain it, except to point out that the field is of an unfamiliar type." Something beeped behind him and he finished as he turned to his insistent console. "The knowledge responsible for such an impressive piece of physics must be formidable."

He paused, then: "Sensors indicate we are now being probed."

"Captain," Walking Bear exclaimed as he switched back to longer-range scanners, "there it is!"

No gasps issued from those on the Bridge. They'd seen too many wonders on too many worlds to be easily overwhelmed. But the bow view offered of the approaching craft was radical and unexpected enough to set speculation rife in their minds even at this distance.

At first it resembled the face of a demon. Nearness resolved hazy lines into the struts and projections of a real ship—of peculiar design, but a ship nonetheless.

The demon's face was formed by what was probably the command section or bridge. The curving prow formed the rest of the head, while propulsion "wings" hinted at monstrous horns. A round glassy glow the hue of polished onyx was centered in the middle of the construct like a baleful Polyphemian eye.

Every arch, every line of it hinted at an engineering knowledge and sophistication undreamed of by Federation shipwrights. Yet it remained a vessel composed of recognizable sections. One that could have been built by Federation hands if the basic blueprints and knowledge had been supplied.

The command module was unarguably a command module. Propulsion units, winglike or not, could be nothing but propulsion units. All this was evident, despite the differences in size.

"The approaching vessel is slowing," Arex announced laconically into the quiet. "It is . . ."

Only the ship's battle compensators saved everyone on the Bridge from permanent blindness as pure radiance struck forward.

The vibration died slowly and there was a distant mutter of thunder as air somewhere within the ship was displaced. Kirk didn't need instruments to tell him what had happened.

They had been fired on by an energy weapon of a new type and of considerable power—and they had been hit point blank. Port and starboard scanners locked on the alien as it fired again.

Coruscating breakers of fire foamed across the forward edge of the cruiser's saucer decks and organized confusion reigned on the Bridge as all alert indicators on board flashed crimson.

Half asleep, off-shift personnel who had been awakened before by the severe shaking wondered what was happening as they scrambled for their duty clothes and stations.

"Full power all shields . . . all engines, maximum reverse thrust!" Kirk was shouting at Walking Bear. "Try to get us away from that beam!" Even as he finished, another blast of intense energy rocked the battered ship.

Amid the confusion and harried reactions and semipanic, rose the calm, steady voice of Spock. "Evasive action will not be effective, Captain. The forcefield now surrounding us is ninety-eight point two percent efficient. Our maneuverability is severely limited."

"Maneuvering be hanged!" Kirk cursed as much in

frustration as anger. "If that thing can fire in, maybe we can fire out. Mr. Walking Bear, lock main phasers on that ship and fire. Arex, our field of movement appears to be restricted. That means you're going to have to use your imagination to avoid that energy beam."

Ayes echoed from both stations.

The Edoan navigator embarked upon what Kirk later described as a maneuvering miracle. Using only impulse power to minimize stress-threat to the main engines, he managed to shift the cruiser's position within the confined area of the force globe so often and so unpredictably that it suffered only glancing blows from the irresistible energy beam.

At the same time the *Enterprise*'s phasers began to reply with lambent salvos of its own. The destructive double beams sought outward.

Kirk's hopes died when they reached no farther than the interior curve of the pale blue field, where the concentrated energy simply stopped.

"Dispersed, possibly, within the fabric of the field itself," Spock theorized.

Walking Bear continued to fire, but their phasers proved totally ineffective even as the white flame continued to lick at their deflector shields.

"The force globe is selective," Spock commented dispassionately, lending voice to the obvious. "Our attacker can beam us at will and we are helpless to respond."

Kirk mulled this over furiously, hunting for a flaw in the alien's seeming invincibility. They couldn't absorb much more of this intense punishment without overloaded deflectors burning out.

While a force-field is hypothetically capable of dispersing energy among its own fabric, he thought, it is not necessarily effective against more primitive weaponry. Physical objects, for example, possess different properties than those of phaser beams.

He was about to order a full complement of photon torpedoes fired, when the till now unceasing assault unexpectedly stopped. The shaking halted concurrently with the disappearance of the white beam. Behind him, Kirk could hear Uhura struggling to handle the flood of inquiries and reports that started pouring in from every deck and section.

While thankful for the respite, he still remained poised for the barrage to resume at any moment. After all, their best attempts at resistance had already proven childishly weak.

Yet ... the alien had apparently elected to halt its attack. Why? "Cease firing," he ordered, suddenly aware that in the absence of any orders to stop, Walking Bear was persisting in a futile attempt to strike at the belligerent opponent with phasers.

Kirk turned to Spock as the ensign acknowledged the command. "Status on the alien?"

"Still approaching, Captain," Spock told him, his attention fixed on his instruments. "Going sub-light now. It has continued probing us throughout the battle ... a moment." He paused, then, "Its surrounding energy pattern is now shifting.".

As they watched in amazement, the field of intense radiance which hugged the alien craft like a tenuous remora, the same field which had first attracted Spock's attention, began to assume density and color. The hull of the craft remained unaltered as this process accelerated, though it grew increasingly difficult to detect through the darkening fog.

It wasn't long before the fashioning of the ghost was finished. The result was so nearly terrestrial that for a moment Kirk almost suspected the "alien's" ancestry.

But no ... it was similar, but undeniably different. The relationship was one of marriage and not blood. That made it no less startling.

The alien's prow had become a huge snake skull. Jaws hung agape and sported gigantic fangs which curved downward and back. It wore a crest of rainbow-hued feathers vaguely resembling the leathery neck shield of the terran South Pacific frilled lizard. Simulated feathers likewise cloaked the propulsion pods, the illusion heightened by the already winglike construction of the engines themselves. Feathers they were not, only brilliantly colored spines of energy, exquisite in their insubstantiality.

Of all the crew, Walking Bear was the most astonished. Nor did he try to conceal it, staring in open-mouthed awe at the fiery image resplendent on the screen, the bizarre craft draped in the ethereal raiment of a serpentine spirit.

"Ever seen anything like that, Spock?" Kirk asked. The heady apparition was baroquely impressive. But the captain had little time for idle admiration, however. His immediate concerns were more basic.

What were the motives behind such blind hostility—and what was the explanation for this at once juvenile and overpowering display? Exactly how the energy sculpture was accomplished was a question he'd leave for Spock.

The difference between captain and science officer, as usual, was the difference between *Why* and *How*.

Spock was elucidating, "It is not Vulcan-inspired, Captain. Nor do I believe it to be of Klingon or Romulan origin. Romulan, possibly, but . . ."

"I recognize it," a voice whispered unexpectedly.

Even Spock showed signs of astonished surprise as everyone on the bridge looked blankly at Walking Bear. The ensign mouthed the word as he continued gazing at the screen.

"Kukulkan."

"The name means nothing to me, Mr. Walking Bear," Kirk pressed when the ensign gave no sign of elaborating.

"Incoming transmission, Cap—"

Uhura never finished the words.

X

The strange, reverberant voice rolled thunderously over the bridge. It was loud, overbearing—but not unbearable—a unique meld as of many voices speaking in unison. Melodious and rhythmic, passionate and forceful, it compelled attention. Kirk stared at the viewscreen image. He began to suspect that it was the ship itself—the ship and its enveloping ghost—that was speaking.

"I attacked you because I believed you had forgotten me. But there is one among you who knows my name."

Kirk shook his head, trying to clear it of the aural cobwebs surrounding the transmission. The voice was engulfed in a swarm of echoes. It was hard to believe there was nothing wrong with his hearing. He found he could force himself to focus on one part of that multifaceted tone. When he did so he could make out the words, distinct and solemn—and threatening.

"You will be given one more chance to succeed where your ancestors failed. Fail me again and all of your kind shall perish!"

The broadcast concluded as abruptly as it had begun.

"Short and sweet," Kirk murmured. But without any of the explanations he so desperately needed. Now he had all this biblical-sounding business of failing ancestors and incipient annihilation to contend with. What were they supposed to have succeeded at, and how had they failed, and whose ancestors did the voice mean, anyhow? His . . . Spock's . . . maybe Arex's or those of M'ress's Caitian system.

If the ghost-maker wanted to play God, the least he could do was be a bit more informative . . .

One thing Kirk *did* know—they were pinioned here by a powerful energy bubble fashioned by an enemy whose actions and words were far from friendly. Before he could decide on a course of action, he had to have facts, information, something on which to hang a supposition. The sole possible source of such information appeared to be a half-green ensign of no combat experience, but with considerable promise.

As Spock returned to his instrumentation and Uhura to communications, Kirk rose from the command chair and walked over to the helm. The subject of his impending—perhaps crucial—questions was sitting silently, apparently thinking hard. But he glanced up readily when Kirk approached.

Kirk started talking in an unintentionally suspicious tone, which he hurriedly corrected. "Mr. Walking Bear, how do you happen to recognize *anything* about that ship?"

For a split second something very old and very wise flashed in the young helmsman's eyes. Then it was gone, and Kirk couldn't be certain afterward if he'd actually seen it.

"I'm an Amerind, Captain. North America territory, desert—southwest, Comanche tribe. Anthropology's always been a hobby of mine—personal anthropology in particular." He smiled, ever so slightly.

"You have to know, Captain, that I was an example of an almost extinct terran subspecies . . . the orphan. So I'm rather more interested in my own history than most people. In the course of pursuing my own past, I've also had occasion to study the history of many earlier Earth cultures. Now the image assumed by that ship out there," he gestured at the screen, "bears a powerful resemblance to a god in ancient Aztec legends—Kukulkan. The variance is minimal . . . shockingly so."

Despite the factual knowledge to the contrary, there were still times when Kirk couldn't be sure which was the faster . . . the library computer or its master. In any case, Spock spoke up almost immediately.

"Captain, the records confirm Ensign Walking Bear's suspicions. The countenance of the alien is a remarkable analog of the Central American deity Kukulkan. Research shows that the Aztecs and their neighbors and predecessors—the Mayas and Toltecs, Zapotecs, Olmecs and many others—all possessed legends of a winged serpent god."

He nodded toward the screen. "Ensign Walking Bear does not carry his information far enough, however." A quick glance at the readouts produced more startling information. "It seems that many other cultures besides the Indian of Central America include stories of a winged serpent in their mythologies. The Chinese, for example, and many African tribes. He is referred to most often as a wise but terrible god, a bringer of knowledge and . . ."

"Myoka Mbowe."

"What's that?" Kirk spun, to face the communications station.

"*Hmmm?*" Uhura snapped out of her daydream. "Sorry, Captain. When I was a little girl, my grandmother used to tell me all the old handed-down fairy tales. Some of the stories revolved around the exploits of a god called Myoka Mbowe. It translates roughly from the Swahili as *winged snake*."

"It is clear, Captain," Spock continued, "that such legends were abundant among Earth's primitive societies."

"So that explains it," Kirk muttered, turning back to the viewscreen. "We've been attacked by a myth." His voice rose slightly. "A terran philosopher once said that there are no myths, only vague distortions of half-remembered truths.

"We could be dealing here with the basis of all those legends, all those millennia-old stories—a space traveler who visited Earth in ancient times."

Spock nodded. "Entirely possible."

"It's not possible," objected Arex. "How can we be dealing with the same ship or traveler who forms the base for such legends? That would make the being in question many thousands of years old."

"A possibility," Spock observed solemnly, "which cannot be discounted."

"I'll even grant the chance of that, Spock," Kirk allowed, "if you'll tell me what all this business of destroying us, and failing, and ancestor ineffectuality is about? I just can't understand such naked hatred."

Spock had turned back to the quiet scrutiny of his instruments. "I have no doubt that in time, we will be duly informed . . ."

Soft sound heavy sound . . . the bass engine of a human heart. It sounded clear and regular from the sensor amplifier that was only a tiny part of the incredibly complex diagnostic bed.

Always astonishing, that one muscle on which everything hinges, isn't it, Bones? He studied the figure prone before him.

The sophisticated bed monitoring equipment needed little in the way of external confirmation, but playing safe as always, he passed the belt medicorder over the crewman's forehead. A quick check to insure that the readings matched, and then he laid it back on the nearby table.

"You don't deserve it, specialist," he told the waiting youth gruffly, "but you're getting a few days bed rest."

The security specialist managed a slight smile. One hand gingerly felt the ear McCoy had treated. "It's not necessary, Dr. McCoy. I can handle my duties."

"Mine too? I'll do the prescribing around here. A few days bed rest. Remember, arguing with a superior officer is *almost* as bad as arguing with a doctor. And the next time you get the urge for some off-shift exercise, I suggest you try something besides high-diving into a minimum-level pool."

"Don't worry, Doctor," the specialist cringed. "I had to learn the hard w—" His mouth opened wide.

While the pain in his ear had abated under McCoy's skillful ministrations, it now seemed as if his other faculties had been affected for the worse.

Certainly his eyes were hardest hit, because he could swear that McCoy had become enveloped in a stuttering, immobilizing light, as though attacked by a turquoise strobe. It froze McCoy next to the bed without touching his patient.

It seemed that the flickering light appeared and died faster and faster. It seemed that McCoy was trying to say something. It seemed that Dr. McCoy had vanished.

The . . .

Scott was alone in the jeffries tube. He was inspecting the circuitry which ran from the great warp-drive engines to the engineering computer.

Actually, it was a job any engineering tech could have handled. But when the usual twelve desperate crises weren't clamoring for his immediate attention, Scott always made time for carrying out some of the more routine tasks of engineering maintenance by himself. It was always beneficial, he felt, for an experienced engineer to immerse himself in the plebeian from time to time, to work with a fluid-state hydrometer instead of giving orders.

And besides, he enjoyed it.

Running the tricorder across yet another opened panel cover gave him the same feeling of aesthetic enjoyment, the same emotional satisfaction as he followed micro-chips and coupled modules, that another man might have found in a painting by Turner or a Brahms symphony. Such diffuse and openly gushing creations would have as little appeal to him as to Spock. Scott's artistic tastes were well suited to his profession—Escher for art, say, and Stockhausen in music.

He refastened the panel and prepared to run the compact instrument over the next one. The radiance which enveloped him as he started upward was the blue of a Baja sky.

Then he was gone, the tricorder crying out hollowly for him as it clattered and pinged its way down the open passage . . .

The Four . . .

Kirk paced the deck in front of the command chair. It was simplistic and unscientific; and like many simplistic and unscientific remedies, it worked. He wondered who the first human was who discovered that one of the better salves for the harried mind lay in the feet.

"There's got to be a solution to this deadlock," he was mumbling. "Probably right in front of our eyes." He turned toward the helm. "Mr. Walking Bear, what do the legends say about . . ."

Walking Bear dissolved in a rain of blue gas followed by a tiny bang as a puff of air rushed in to occupy the space formerly displaced by the ensign.

As if he could snatch him back from an unknown fate, Kirk rushed the seat. But the helmsman was gone. To make sure, Kirk moved his hands through the air above the helm seat. No, the body of Walking Bear hadn't been made invisible—it had been made absent.

The Four Are . . .

"Captain," a hesitant voice called. Still dazed by this new development, Kirk turned to face Uhura. She sounded equally stunned, almost apologetic. "Security reports from both Sick Bay and Engineering. Both Dr. McCoy and Chief Engineer Scott have disappeared.

"No one saw Mr. Scott vanish. We have a report on Dr. McCoy's disappearance, however. Apparently he was administering treatment to an injured security specialist . . ." she paused a moment to listen, "Jo van Dreenan, at the time. He claims that Dr. McCoy was held motionless within a blue haze, then he vanished, just like . . ." She nodded toward the now empty helm chair.

Kirk turned to the main viewscreen, where the ghostly alien still hovered directly ahead. There was as much curiosity as anger in his question.

"What are they, or it, doing to my crew?"

A thorough visual demonstration negates the necessity for words. The pulsating blue amoeba ingested Kirk, flickered briefly, and took him, too.

"Captain!" Spock shouted. There was no response. Now the first officer's gaze likewise turned to the viewscreen, and he thought things which, while not exactly emotional, were far from flattering.

But though he wished it aloud among the imprecations, the blue light did not reappear to take him too
. . .

The Four Are Chosen.

A vast, gray plain, open and desolate. Dull gray ground reaching to a featureless horizon, melting into a sky the color of antimony. Color began to brighten one tiny bit of it.

The four did not appear simultaneously. And although McCoy was the first chosen, he was not the first to appear. That privilege was reserved for Walking Bear. He was followed by Scott, then Kirk, and the good doctor last of all.

This sequence was intentional and proper. It was not, as a human observer might guess, executed at random. It was only that Kukulkan's science made use of space-time theorems that Scott would have sneered at.

Lead landscape and dirty-cotton hills, rippling rain-laden sky without moisture. Gray pseudopods of rippling gray lakes. It was as drab as an idle thought.

Each man reacted with differing degrees of surprise and alarm as he rematerialized. No one stopped to analyze whether it was instinct or common sense that prompted them to move close to one another, their backs to a common center.

Kirk was the first to recover and commence examining their surroundings. As soon as he had perceived that there was no immediate threat to their continued existence, his powerful curiosity had taken over. He was already gauging their chances for escape . . . even though he had no specific idea where they were.

Generally, however, he felt safe in commenting: "We're somewhere inside the other ship." Silence from his three companions indicated they shared that opinion.

It was absolutely silent in that unimaginative arena. No breeze ruffled the atmosphere.

"No cover," Scott noted. "And us without a single phaser or communicator between us."

"I have a suspicion neither would be of much use, Scotty."

"That may be so, Captain, but I'd settle for a nice, ineffective laser cannon all the same. Purely as a psychological prop, of course."

Kirk smiled faintly. "Me too, Scotty."

McCoy was looking down at himself and patting his waist. "I've still got my belt medikit, for all the good that's worth."

"I hope you won't have to use it, Bones."

"Hold on." Scott looked puzzled. "I had an engineering tricorder with me. It must have remained behind on the ship when I was brought over. So why weren't Dr. McCoy's medical 'corder and supplies interfered with?"

"Where was it, Scotty?"

"Right in my fist, Captain. I was inspecting some circuitry with it."

Kirk shrugged. "That might explain it. Probably the instruments that were monitoring our transport read Bones' kit as part of his clothing, whereas you were more noticeably employing yours as a tool. I don't think you'd find much use for it here."

"Maybe not, Captain," Scott replied, "but then, I'm a full-time believer in the hairpin hypothesis."

"Hairpin hypo ... what's *that?*" McCoy wondered aloud.

"An old engineer's adage that goes way back, Doctor," explained Scott. "It states that 'no tool is so useless that something can't be found it can be used to fix' ... but I'd still rather have a phaser."

"I'm beginning to believe Spock was right about the entity behind all this," Kirk allowed. "That drone probe was unlikely, this ship is unlikely, and its method of communication the most unlikely of all. So I suppose the possibility that we're dealing with a being thousands of years old is no more unlikely than the others have been. When it begins acting rationally, that's when I guess I'll start doubting this." He turned to the youngest of the four.

"Mr. Walking Bear, do the legends say what eventually happened to this Kukulkan? Old cultures usually disposed of their gods neatly."

"Only that he left and promised to return one day, sir."

Kirk looked satisfied. "Sounds like all the promises ascribed to all the ancient gods of Earth." He looked from one to the other. "I don't think we need doubt that the drone probe was an information gatherer for this Kukulkan." He turned pensive.

"I only wish I knew what it was in that information that's caused the receiver to act in such an unfriendly manner, without even giving us a chance to find out what's behind all this. I . . ." He hesitated.

"What is it, Jim?" asked McCoy, sounding worried.

"Listen." They fell silent. In the complete quiet a distant buzz became audible . . . muted but unmistakable. In grew louder, and then familiar.

It was the sound of many tongues speaking simultaneously. It had overtones of pure alienness, which did not bother Kirk at all. It also hinted of expectancy, which did.

"We're being watched, I think," commented McCoy, eyeing the gray bowl of sky uneasily.

"When I was a child," Walking Bear murmured, "I used to hide in a hall closet when I was supposed to be asleep, so I could listen to the adults talking in the sitting room. There wasn't a minute when I wasn't afraid the door would fly open to show my foster mother standing there, glaring down at me, ready to send me to bed with a beating." He studied the featureless plain.

"Strange how the earliest emotions linger the longest."

Kirk faced his chief engineer. "Is there any way Spock could get through to us with a transporter beam?"

"I don't think so, sir," Scott said, shaking his head in resignation. "Our sensors couldn't penetrate this ship's screens. And since our phasers couldn't break out of the energy bubble around the ship, I don't see a transporter beam doin' any better."

The steady buzz intensified. The four men diligently

searched the horizon, at once hoping to see something, and hoping not to. Then the insectlike hum seemed to coalesce. The resulting voice still had touches of many, but now the words were distinct—and comprehensible.

"Now I will show to you the seeds that I have sown before," it pontificated. "Learn from them . . . find the purpose if you can. If you can do so, then and only then will I appear before you."

The buzzing voice faded to nothingness. Even as it was dying away, it was drowned by a profound thunder, as though immense engines were stirring underfoot, in the air, in the gray walls enclosing them.

As Kirk stared and tried not to sweat—there were less elaborate ways of killing four men, and anyway, the voice had said they had some seeds to inspect, whatever that meant—the landscape began to change color. Initially it shifted to an orange-gray. As the concussive rumble mounted, the gray gave way to a pure, almost blinding orange. Distances were indeterminate, but it seemed a sun appeared in open sky above. It was lambent orange. The rumbling reached a peak whereupon definite tones could be heard. They verged on music, but then so did the machinery of a kilometerssquare factory. It was almost, McCoy thought, as if an enormous organ was playing somewhere—woodwind, violin, flute and chime pipes all weaving in and out among the deepest pedal notes. Everything participating, he mused, but a vox humana. He didn't expect to hear anything as comforting as that.

The Ivesian mosaic softened and orange turned to blue. Apparently Kukulkan's usable spectrum differed from theirs.

The result of all the activity began manifesting itself. First the familiar vegetation started to appear. Palm trees, huge ferns, vines and creepers lacing together a network of trees rose from the orange-blue ground. Dense undergrowth filled in the empty places like an afterthought.

It surrounded them on three sides, leaving only the ground directly ahead still barren. A trickle of running water could be heard; but even so, the amazing simulacrum still lacked something.

Kirk fixed on it a moment later. This was a curiously lifeless simulacrum. There were no animal sounds. No birds, no complaining primates . . . not even the addle-pated hum of a hunting wasp. There were no smells, either, of hidden creatures. There should have been the musky odor of mobile life. Instead, there was only the oddly uninviting perfume of huge blossoms, the pungent miasma of steaming greenery.

Nothing. For all its color this fabricated jungle was as dead as the gray womb they had just vacated.

As if in anger, the rumbling sound returned. This time it was accompanied by a violent vibrating which rattled Kirk's teeth and pricked at his spine.

Lines appeared in the open ground before them. This section was mostly lower than the slight rise they stood on, and Kirk could see rectangles and squares being laid out on the orange. Something was tracing a city there.

It began to sprout, weedlike, from the porous ground.

Had he overlooked the possibility that they had been transported to some far world, and there ensconced in a clay cavern? No . . . the structures forming in front of him were made of something similar to, but far more sophisticated than clay. Then he recognized it—the material was almost identical to the strange crystalline substance of the alien's hull.

Hints of many cultures were embodied in those buildings: touches of Mayan architecture, Aztec edification, of Egyptian engineering and Southeast Asian religious construction and a host of a hundred others. Not all were extinct, but all were distinct. Yet they blended in a way which suggested that this fabrication and not the aged realities was the end to which they had all been striving.

Fragmentary Sumer merged with oil-age New York baroque. Bits of Inca regularity were subsumed by the curves of dead Monomotapa. Everything was enmeshed in its neighbor, interwoven and entwined and interchanged.

Despite this, the commandments of basic geometry held court, and somehow it all worked.

The city seemed livable, if not downright inviting. Nor did it appear all that primitive. Some of the angles and reflective buttresses were unrecognizable even to Scott's experienced eye.

The chief engineer was more interested in the material than in the method. It looked like ordinary stone ... but when the sun struck a wall or parapet at a certain angle, the hard reflection that resulted was more suited to polished metal. And if you squinted a little with your eyes—and mind—various structures seemed built of opaque glass.

What could only be the city's entrance lay immediately before them, an open gate flanked by two sleek cylindrical towers. They resembled Egyptian obelisks. Yet when the light changed a little it was clear they were akin to the great towers once raised by the mystic artist-architects of Mohenjo Daro.

Just as Kirk was convinced the construction was complete, the persistent rumble rose almost painfully in volume. As the ground quaked underfoot, a single colossal structure leaped skyward from the city center. Dominating the skyline, it seemed to pull all the lines of each and every building, every tower and wall, together to form an unbreakable metropolitan whole. It was the highest facet on a well-cut gem.

As the final block appeared, and the last decoration materialized on the walls, the rumbling sound died for the final time.

The four officers were left to stand and wonder at a city at once alien and familiar. And no wonder, for it was the city man had almost raised half a hundred times, all across his world. The city that shows up in the corner of an architect's eye but never seems the same when committed to blueprint ... the city men see in old dreams ...

As if any more was necessary, here was yet further proof that whatever else this Kukulkan was, he was not an entity to be mocked.

There was much care and purpose behind all this display. Despite the near cataclysmic threats inherent in that many-toned voice, Kirk couldn't help but feel a certain thrill of expectation at imminent revelations of the highest import. Within that city might lie explanations for all the mythologies of mankind.

That would not please some people.

"I've never seen anything quite like it, Captain," Scott murmured appreciatively at the eerie beauty of it, "not in all my landfalls on many worlds."

"What's behind it, though?" wondered McCoy.

Kirk spoke thoughtfully. "The voice spoke of seeds and unfulfilled deeds, Bones. An enormous puzzle's been set before us. Let's start inspecting the pieces."

They headed for the city gate. . . .

An assistant engineer was aiding Spock as the first officer worked at Scott's Bridge engineering station. Another technician stood ready nearby, to respond to muted commands with information or manipulation of certain instruments.

Sulu was at the helm now, the position vacated so startlingly by Ensign Walking Bear. All stations, in fact, were double-manned back throughout the *Enterprise,* as it remained on red alert. Everyone knew that the captain and three others had been taken. No one would sleep until their fate was known.

While the force-field enclosing them gave no sign of weakening, Spock wanted to be ready should their still unknown assailant give them the slightest chance to break free.

He concluded his operations at the engineering station and crossed back toward his own.

Uhura chose that moment to voice the concern which had been building in her for many minutes. "Mr. Spock, shouldn't we be trying to find out what's become of the captain, Dr. McCoy and the others?"

"Lieutenant Uhura, you are supposed to be monitoring the alien vessel for any possible incoming communiqués. You know that our first priority is to free the *Enterprise* and ourselves. As soon as that is accomplished, we can attend to the release of all kidnapped personnel. Continue with your regular duties."

"Yes, sir," she muttered. Spock began recalling information from the library. She continued to stare at him for a long moment and then returned her attention to her own console. She might have been muttering something under her breath. Then again, she might not. Uhura could be unreadable at times.

Four men stood almost respectfully before the towering spires guarding the city's central boulevard. Close inspection convinced Kirk that they *were* Egyptian obelisks.

"With at least one significant difference, sir," Walking Bear exclaimed.

Kirk remembered that Walking Bear was only an amateur anthropologist. He wished for Spock's more definitive explanations. But Spock wasn't here. In his absence, they would have to depend on the ensign's informal readings. So far, though, he had to admit, the young helmsman's observations had been as accurate as anyone could wish.

"It's those carvings, sir," Walking Bear was explaining as he pointed to incisions about three meters off the ground on the nearest tower.

Kirk eyed them.

They had been exquisitely rendered by a careful, expert hand, he would have said, had he not seen the entire city raised from—*not the dust, Kirk,* he warned himself. *Don't get biblical—you've encountered races with matter-manipulation abilities before.*

He couldn't identify the style of carving. The subjects seemed uncomplicated, though. Animals and people from many different countries and regions of ancient Earth.

"Notice that one there, sir," Walking Bear suggested. "The third row over, first on the bottom."

Kirk found the indicated carving and instantly understood why the ensign attached such significance to it. It bore an uncanny resemblance to the ghost image which now cloaked Kukulkan's ship, that of a feathered serpent. In this particular rendition the wings were spread wider, and the body was coiled. It hovered over a lifelike flurry of little cuts which could only be water.

"No Egyptian ever carved anything like that, sir."

Kirk nodded, indicated they should continue on.

They passed through the gate, which Scott claimed closely approximated some ruins he'd encountered in old China. For his part, Walking Bear maintained that the wall braces backing the towers and arch overhead could only be Scythian in origin.

"Can't pin it down," he finally confessed. "It's like the rest of this place, only on a smaller scale. There's that weird blend of many unrelated civilizations again."

"Everything's a clue, Walking Bear," said Kirk. "Remember, this city is intended to be one gigantic riddle. If nothing seems to belong to its neighbor, that must be significant, too."

The avenue they were walking down was wide and well paved with blocks composed of that same strange stone-metal-glass mix. They continued down it for what felt like a fair distance, examining each structure in turn as they passed it. Every one was finished down to the tiniest detail. Painstaking care had been exercised in this gargantuan recreation, which in turn was part of some still unknown charade.

It was the less amiable McCoy who finally called a halt to the seemingly endless hike. "Okay, so we're here—so, what are we supposed to do now?"

"Your opinion, Mr. Walking Bear?"

The ensign looked at him in surprise. He suspected the captain's growing confidence in him; he was used to offering opinions to the computer in study center, in response to queries posed in technical manuals—not to the ship's captain. For a moment he could only gawk helplessly.

"Come on, Ensign," Kirk finally urged, sensing the other's lack of assurance. "We're all of us equally on trial here."

"Sir, I . . . I haven't the faintest idea what we're expected to do."

"Just tell me what comes to you," Kirk soothed. "Tell us more about Kukulkan . . . maybe something useful will surface." He smiled encouragingly.

Walking Bear grinned slightly. "Well . . . before he left, the legends say Kukulkan gave the Mayas their remarkably accurate calendar, instructing them to build a great city according to its cycles. On the day the city was finished, he was supposed to return."

As he told the weathered story, the orange-blue sun shone down on them with unvarying warmth, never stirring from its assigned place in the sky.

"The Mayas built their city and waited. Something about it must have been wrong, because Kukulkan never returned. Maybe they paid too much attention to the parts of the calendar that told them the best times for planting corn . . . I don't know.

"They tried again and again . . . at Chichén Itzá, Tulum, Uxmal and others. None induced the god to return." He glanced at the silent structures bordering the avenue. "As Mr. Spock said, many cultures have such legends."

"The history of Earth," Kirk whispered, "is a history of unfulfilled promises," but no one else heard him. He spoke again, more briskly. "Kukulkan must have visited many of those ancient peoples. It appears each used only parts—different parts—of his knowledge to build their own cities."

"Does that mean they were all trying to build something that was supposed to look like this?" McCoy asked.

Walking Bear hedged. "I *think* so, sir, but they all failed. The Mayas used one part, the Indus River civilizations another, the builders of Zimbabwe yet another . . . over and over, failure after failure, the original knowledge growing more and more distorted with each succeeding culture."

"I see," commented McCoy. "An architectural Tower of Babel."

"Sometimes I wonder about us humans, Bones," Kirk murmured. "Someone could come along and hand us the plans for the ultimate civilization—and we'd manage to bollix it up somehow. We're too vain, as a race and as individuals.

"There's always someone who has to improve perfection, just to get his hundredth of a credit in." His voice grew tauter. "Though from what I've seen of this Kukulkan and his methods this far, I wouldn't bet that some farsighted city builders didn't perform a little sabotage on those building instructions."

"Kukulkan said he would appear only when we learned the city's purpose," Walking Bear reminded them. "Unfortunately, none of the legends mention what that purpose was."

Kirk ran his hand over the hair above his neck. "Let's use what facts we have. Supposedly these cities were built to bring Kukulkan back to Earth. How? Obviously he hasn't been hanging around Earth, or anywhere else in our neck of the galaxy for the last several thousand years to see if someone eventually hit it right.

"That means this city has to hold some kind of signaling device." The structures surrounding them took on new meaning. "It can't be too complicated. It has to be something the Egyptians or Mayas could have built, and out of local materials. The basic technology can't be too advanced, either.

"That means we're not going to find any deep-space transmitters housed in a stone pyramid. This Kukulkan's approach to basic physics seems pretty different from our own. I don't see why some simple yet efficient communicating system couldn't utilize equally unorthodox technology.

"It has to be in plain sight, I think. After all, the transmitting machinery is the reason behind building the entire city." He gestured down the street they were on.

"That central pyramid is the city's physical and visual focal point. Seems a good place to start."

In the humid silence of an unlengthening day, they started toward it . . .

XI

Eventually they stood at one corner of the ziggurat, at the intersection of the main boulevard and several smaller avenues. At the center of this modest intersection rose a small tower. It wasn't a very big tower, but that did not detract from its impressiveness. Roughly five meters high, it bore a definite resemblance to the elaborately worked, gilded temple towers of the Southeast Asia sector of Earth.

Rounded and roughly ovoid, it was made up of eight tiers of progressively diminishing size, cut from brightly colored stone. At the top of the spire was a graven image of Kukulkan's head. It was exquisitely executed, finely detailed. Everything looked lifelike—the serpent head with its gaping fanged mouth, the collar of metal and glass feathers around the neck, and the rainbow feathered frill formed of inlaid semiprecious stones.

Tilted up and back, the head stared into the sky at a forty-five degree angle, facing away from the pyramid behind. It wore a baleful expression, at once expectant and commanding.

At the sharp-edged corner of the enormous pyramid, a stairway built to human proportions started upward. As near as they could tell it reached to the top of the massive stone structure. At the moment, though, their attention was held by the impressive sculpture from which the web of roads radiated.

"Funny," Walking Bear was murmuring, hands resting on hips as he studied the sculpture, "I've never seen a representation like this before."

170

Kirk glanced up at the pyramid behind them, then back to his companions. "Since the big pyramid's the center of everything, I'd guess it also has something to do with the answer to everything. Maybe it's at the top. I'm going up. The rest of you spread out and circle it. Try to stay within earshot of each other, within sight if possible. Anyone finds anything that demands immediate evaluation, he gives a holler. *Don't* try operating any levers or doorhandles without calling someone else to help. I don't want anyone vanishing down trick hallways."

"Aye, sir . . . yes, sir . . . okay, Jim," came the replies. Kirk started up the seemingly endless series of steps, while the others split up.

Scott and Walking Bear hadn't gone far to the south before the ensign picked out a distinctive shape far down the walkway. He pointed. "Another tower, I think, sir."

"Come on, lad."

They broke into a trot. As they drew nearer and nearer, they saw that Walking Bear was right. Furthermore, this new structure was more than just another tower . . . it was an exact duplicate of the one they had just encountered.

It lay in the center of another confluence of streets, as had the first. Walking Bear spared it only a glance before strolling out to where he could peer around the pyramid's corner.

Only the unnatural clarity of the air within the huge chamber enabled him to identify the outlines of the dim object in the distance.

"There's a third tower down this way, sir. There must be one at each of the four corners . . ."

Kirk didn't waste energy panting. There was no one around to sympathize. And he had gauged the hike accurately—no difficult task for a man used to estimating astronomical distances. So when he arrived at the top he was more psychologically than physically winded.

He was almost disappointed. The revelation he had hoped for consisted only of a flat, square platform supported on four poles. It perched in unimpressive solitude atop the pyramid. Its sole distinction was that it seemed made of metal—more metal than they'd seen anywhere in the city in one place. But closer inspection failed to disclose the nature of the alloy.

The square itself framed a lustrous, transparent round mosaic depicting Kukulkan in the same coiled, in-flight pose carved on the gate obelisks. The mosaic seemed to be encased in clear quartz, but Kirk didn't trust his initial estimates here. It did look like quartz, though.

He could just see over the top of the platform. There was no question of the mosaic's importance. It was a magnificent piece of craftsmanship, worthy of a fine jeweler, resplendent in its rendering. Other than its opulent beauty, however, it held no attraction for the captain.

Kirk crouched slightly to see beneath the platform. The bottom of the transparent mosaic was as flawless as the top. Passing through it, the rays of the artificial sun cast the winged serpent image clear and sharp on the stone beneath. Dust motes danced in the painted light.

Everything had been arranged here with extreme precision, to produce ... what? Kirk rose and eyed the top of the mosaic once more, looked down at the image it cast on the stone, and considered thoughtfully.

Walking Bear and Scott were absorbed in their inspection of the second ornamental tower. They had negotiated the easy climb and now stood at the top, even with the sculpted serpent head.

Nearness brought knowledge concealed by height. Immediately they noticed two things not visible from ground level.

For one, the eyes of the statue were composed of concentric inlays of some translucent glassy material instead of opaque rock. Of more obvious significance was the faceted prism like some huge gem which was securely positioned at the back of the stone gullet.

Scott's engineering sense was more intrigued by, say, the controls of a ship than its more impressive bulk. Consequently, while Walking Bear was engrossed in deep study of the eyes and prism, his older companion was busily examining the collar of inlaid feathers which circled the statue's neck. He was hunting for imperfections more significant than the perfection, and he found one at the base of the fringed collar.

"Looks like there's a seam here. I think the head is meant to be turned. Come on, lad, give me a hand."

Lining himself up with his hands on the back of the collar, he directed Walking Bear to press in the same clockwise direction with both hands on the lower stone jaw. Together they shoved.

There was a rasp and squeak as of metal on rock . . . or maybe rock on metal, given the peculiar composition of the building materials here.

More important, the head seemed to move a little.

"Try again, lad." Both men strained, using their body weight against the recalcitrant sculpture. Something snapped inside and the head started to turn smoothly on a hidden pivot. As it turned to the sun, the glassy eyes began to glow, to shine with an inner light that appeared far stronger than mere reflection.

Scott and Walking Bear were too absorbed in the effort of turning the head to notice this new development. Fortunately, someone else was in the perfect position to do so.

Even from his high perch the intensity of the glow in the statue's eyes was so commanding that Kirk noticed it immediately. He spun and shielded his own eyes as he stared upward, muttering excitedly to himself.

"Of course . . . the sun! No wonder it hasn't moved . . . the position is crucial to the city riddle." He turned downward and shouted through cupped hands. No wind kidnapped his call.

"Scotty! Turn the head a hundred and eighty degrees, so that it looks up here!"

The chief engineer's voice echoed back faintly. "Aye, sir."

The head had been turned almost completely around when the polished prism in its mouth also began to shine. Simultaneously, the brightness of the inlaid eyes grew so brilliant that Kirk could no longer look directly at them without squinting. As the carved skull ground

the last few degrees, a beam of light suddenly sprang
from the serpent's jaws toward the top of the pyramid.
It was accompanied by a hissing sound that grew rapidly louder.

Kirk had moved clear. Like a reaching arm, the
combined triple beam of eyes and mouth passed
directly before him, between the two nearest poles. It
struck the underside of the mosaic held carefully suspended by the metal platform. The result was marvelous and unexpected.

As the nearly solid light from below struck the mosaic and passed through it, steady explosions of glittering energy formed in the air directly above, forming
and bursting and bursting and forming like bubbles in
champagne.

The hissing became a nervous crackling sound. It reminded Kirk of an incomplete electrical connection—
though nothing so simple was at work here. Below,
Walking Bear and Chief Scott stared anxiously upward,
awaiting word from Kirk.

They could see the glow at the top of the pyramid,
the distant figure of the captain silhouetted before it.
But at this distance they couldn't tell anything else. A
moment later and they were reassured as the diminu-
tive form called down to them.

"Turn the other heads this way," the voice ordered.
Scott yelled acknowledgment, and both men started
down from the tower.

As soon as he saw them moving, Kirk edged around
to the other side of the platform area, carefully avoid-
ing the beam. He spotted McCoy waiting patiently by
the base of the fourth tower.

"Bones! The serpent's head—turn it to face the pyramid! I'm coming down."

The stone skull was heavy . . . too heavy for one
man. McCoy was still struggling with it when Walking
Bear and Scott got the second head moving.

Again the tongue of light leaped upward to strike at
the pyramid's apex. Now they could hear the crackling
sound as it intensified with the addition of this second
source of power, see the color of the strange energy
deepen.

It remained for Kirk to give McCoy a hand in turning the next head. That finished, they climbed down and headed for the remaining sculpture. All four men met at the last tower, the one they had originally encountered.

For the fourth time the procedure was performed, sending a beam of intense light upward. The top of the pyramid, as Scott and Walking Bear descended, was now completely engulfed by the sphere of pure energy roiling angrily above it.

Abruptly the crackling hiss gave way to a thunderous rumbling, utterly unlike the sound which had accompanied the raising of the city. It dropped in volume, deepened until it seemed as if the very fabric of existence was being punctured by that glittering ball.

Streaks of pure light occasionally shot lightninglike through the multihued nimbus as it continued to grow and expand.

Below, the four officers had to shield their eyes as the glow from the top of the pyramid intensified to where it was greater than the sun.

"The whole thing," Kirk yelled as a breeze sprang up strongly around them, whipping at uniforms and hair, "is some kind of energy amplification device based on solar power—Kukulkan's special signal!"

The tenor of the rumbling changed to a steady drone as the energy ball began a steady pulsing. That's when the voices returned. Many voices joined as one. But this time the stentorian sussuration sounded even above the pulsating signal, reverberated until the multiple distortions were sloughed off like dead thoughts.

Gradually, the many whispers solidified until what they heard was, for the first time, unmistakably the voice of a single being.

"After scores of centuries," the voice boomed, "my design has been fulfilled. Behold me, then, as I am!"

The energy globe vanished in an air-splitting explosion. McCoy and Scott were both thrown to the ground. Kirk managed to grab the tower for support, while Walking Bear somehow succeeded in maintaining his balance.

The last flicker of energy was gone, dissipated in the

magnificence of its own disruption by a force still greater. In its place was a hovering, fluttering form that was at once terrifying and beautiful. It was garbed in a cloak of glowing light. Huge membranous wings beat the air as it drifted above the pyramid. Multicolored, scaled torso coiling and recoiling reflexively, neck plumage shifting through a rainbow of brilliance, the massive shape stared down at them. Dragon tongue darted in and out of fanged maw, while dragon eyes glared past flaring nostrils.

"Behold Kukulkan," the apparition rumbled, still enveloped by now dimmed light from the four energy beams. Kirk listened and studied, trying to read the motivation masked by those crimson eyes.

"Where are your weapons of destruction?" came the next query. "Use them on me if you dare!"

"Very impressive, if a bit theatrical," McCoy commented phlegmatically. He'd discovered long ago that no matter how powerful or malign an adversary, if one regarded it merely as an anatomical problem to be mentally dissected, the commoner fears could be conveniently laid aside.

His mind was also occupied with hunting for the reasons behind this unnecessarily overwhelming display.

It was Kirk who answered, however. "We have no weapons with us . . . as you undoubtedly know. If we did, we'd use them only with reason. We haven't been given such a reason yet."

The monster threshed air, wings beating angrily. The energy cloak which clung to him ran through the visible spectrum.

"Reasons? Reasons . . . Where is your hate, then? Is that not reason enough? You hate me, do you not? Why then do you not speak to me of your hate?"

Kirk didn't know how to feel. Threatened? No—he was only puzzled. Despite its amply demonstrated power, there was a pathos about this creature he couldn't quite isolate. But that didn't permit him to lower his guard for a second.

"We don't hate you. You fired your weapons at my ship. We fired back."

The energy belt turned deep, furious purple and he added hurriedly. "We acted in self-defense—if you understand the term.

"I am your master!" the serpent roared. "I may do with you as I will, when I wish."

Madder and madder, Kirk mused, his thoughts awhirl. Obviously this entire display was concocted to intimidate them. But this would-be god had aimed at humans of a bygone age, men of less experienced times and readier belief in the supernatural. His words only made those standing below him angry.

"You think we belong to you?" McCoy exclaimed. "We're not part of the furniture of your cold gray house, Kukulkan."

"Aye, and don't plan to be," Scott added.

Kirk spoke quietly, firmly. "Bones, Scotty—don't antagonize it."

"Antagonize it?" Scott argued. "Captain, it's not exactly in a friendly frame of mind right now."

"It is as I thought," the serpent muttered, "you have forgotten me and strayed from the path I set for you."

Kirk spread his arms. The gesture was a plea for information, not mercy. "You say we've forgotten you. How then can you expect us to *worship* you properly, if we don't remember you and know nothing of the path of which you speak? Are we expected to suffer for the transgressions of ancestors dead these many generations?"

To his relief, this was so reasonable sounding that it appeared to have a mollifying effect on the snake-god. It settled to the top of the pyramid.

"There is some truth in your words. You do not know me. Therefore it is my task to teach you."

That worried Kirk some. He had no idea what was meant by teaching here. One thing he was certain of: judging from what they knew of this alien's character so far instruction might not be too pleasant.

As they watched, the atmosphere turned turquoise— the same blue haze that had lifted them from the *Enterprise*. It enveloped everything around them—pyramid, tower, city and jungle.

When the blue fog cleared, and their vision with it,

they found themselves standing in a large, high-ceil-inged room. The city was gone. The room seemed to stretch off to infinity, optical illusion though Kirk knew it must be. Kukulkan's science was unpredictable, but he didn't think it extended to creating infinite space aboard a ship of finite dimensions.

Everything was rounded and curved, smooth here as the city had been sharp-angled. The room itself was well-lit and shaded a deep, rich purple.

Levels and platforms hung scattered throughout the room without any visible support. Set on and around them were dozens of transparent cubicles ... round, square, oddly shaped. More of the same glasslike cages rested on the floor of the chamber.

The whole arrangement was curiously ... curi-ously—Kirk struggled for the right word—sterilized. Yes, hard and sterile.

No bars or force barriers of recognizable type were evident. Some of the containers held plants, others ani-mals. Many of both were unknown to the widely traveled senior officers. Each cage had a pair of thick cables running from it. The cables disappeared into floor or ceiling.

Other wild vegetation grew out in the open, uncaged. Kukulkan was nowhere to be seen.

"Just once," McCoy grumbled, "I wish he'd let us use the stairs."

Kirk examined the incredible collection. "Everything in here is designed to be looked at. I think the idea is that we do some looking."

He selected one path at random among the cubicles and they started down.

"What the devil is this place?" Scott wondered.

"Looks like some kind of zoo," a dubious McCoy commented.

He walked over to one of the glassy cages and tenta-tively felt of the surface. His hand drew back in sur-prise. Despite the glassy sheen, the wall had a greasy feel.

This particular cage housed a creature that resembled a hallucinatory vision of a giant platypus. It surged and heaved about within, obviously oblivious to their presence and as near as they could tell, perfectly happy.

"There're a lot of species here I don't recognize, Jim," McCoy told him.

"Me too, Bones. Species—I don't even recognize some of the environments. Look at that one."

The cage he indicated was filled with a red gas holding pink spongy globules in suspension. Within this atmosphere swam—or flew—a spotted yellow disk encircled with cilia. It looked blankly toward them with four eyes sporting double pupils.

Abruptly (but not unexpectedly) they were joined by another observer. Kukulkan hovered slightly above them and to one side. None of the men moved closer.

But when the serpent spoke the cordiality in its voice was in startling contrast to the violence it had displayed on their confrontation at the pyramid.

"Please feel free to examine any of my specimens."

Specimens? What did this awesome assemblage of life portend? Another mystery they would have to pry out of Kukulkan.

Scott, however, had long since put aside diplomacy in favor of honesty. He shook his head sadly as he surveyed the endless rows of cubicles. "I could never be proud of putting wee beasties in cages. We've long since abandoned such barbarism on Earth."

Kirk glared at his chief engineer, but Kukulkan took no offense.

"All these here lead a peaceful, healthy life. One that is safe and contented."

McCoy had strolled over to a nearby cage. Now he indicated its occupant—a furry, multilegged ball. It was plucking tiny grapelike fruit from a small bush.

"Contented? Cramped in these little cages?"

"Ah, but what you cannot see," the drifting alien explained, "is that each creature is *mentally* in its own natural environment. The fields of the mind are infinite," he concluded profoundly, as McCoy bent to examine the cables leading out of the cage. They ran from the floor into an uninformative, featureless black box attached to the cubicle base.

"They eat, breathe and exist," Kukulkan continued, "in worlds dreamed up by my machines. Worlds that only they can see. Nor do they see you. Nothing is permitted to disturb their satisfying, endless vistas. Each lives its own ideal dream. They do not know they are in cages."

"A cage is a cage no matter how padded the bars," Scott whispered.

Kukulkan's hearing was far from godlike, the chief engineer had long since decided. Nor could he read minds. Otherwise he would have dealt with Scott back at the pyramid.

"Then the city whose puzzle we solved," Walking Bear exclaimed in a sudden burst of realization, "wasn't really there!"

"It was 'there'," Kukulkan informed them, "because I wished it so, for you, and me.

"Each of my specimens has a world of its own far greater than the puny city I created for you."

"I'd hardly call your city our natural environment," Kirk pointed out.

Huge wings struck at the air. "It was meant to be! That beautiful city and all else I taught to your ancestors were intended to be yours. But they became evil and forgetful and imposed their own teachings above mine until the greater was forgotten!"

There was nothing more to be gained by tact, Kirk decided. It was time to try directness. "We don't like being referred to as property," he said.

He was about fed up with this deranged mechanical wizard. To many primitive terran cultures he might well have seemed a god, but a god he was not.

"No one being," Kirk continued, "not even you, has the right to interfere with the natural development of other civilizations. This is a rule we have established for ourselves."

Huge linear muscles contracted, tightened. Wings beat furiously at cages and plants as the serpent flew into a frenzy, eyes bulging, mouth agape. They backed away from such naked rage.

"Do not speak to *me* of development and interference! Do not speak to me of what is *right!* I have been ever alone. Destruction descended on my kind before your race had discovered fire . . . nay, before it learned to lift itself from the mud and walk upright. Is there 'right' in such endless solitude?"

He gestured at several nearby cages. One contained a creature much like an undernourished seal, the other a quivering mass of green and black protoplasm. Between lay xenariums filled with exotic flora.

"Creatures like these have been my only companions for many millennia. I have seen minds like yours on many worlds ... savage, warlike, filled with self-hate and destructive intelligence. You end by destroying yourselves and everything around you, by reducing whole planets to lifeless cinders. After endless encounters with such sickening civilizations I decided to"—the word came out savagely—"interfere! As a hopeful experiment I visited your Earth, among other worlds, and tried to teach peaceful ways to the now vanished cultures of many races.

"Then I left, intending when summoned to return to give you the additional knowledge which would enable you to join me as true equals. But you never sent for me. None did, to whom I gave the knowledge of the city. Finally I sent a probe to find out what had happened. What did it tell me, what did it discover? Warriors!" He spun rapidly in tight circles.

"Still warriors, ever warriors—the same as always. The same as I've seen on half a hundred worlds, only this time more terribly equipped than ever, with yet greater instruments of destruction. You've surpassed the stage of quarreling among yourselves and have carried annihilation to the stars. You will end by destroying the universe!"

"Saints preserve us," murmured a flabbergasted Scott, "a paranoid god."

"But we work only to create peace," Walking Bear objected.

The serpent glared down at them, his shadow darkening the room, wings fluttering in agitation. "Nothing you have done so far makes me believe that is so. I—I have done better."

Again the broad, sweeping gesture, this time taking in the entire horizonless chamber: cages full of snaillike plants, plantlike snails, a cubicle lined with tiny colored balls, animals that resembled rocks, plants that resembled buildings, plant-animals like nothing on Earth.

"My creatures here have little intelligence, yet even the most violent among them exist peacefully in the worlds that I have to give."

Wings moved, and he backed around a corner. They followed cautiously to where an unusually large cage floated in midair. It held an enormous feline creature that was all teeth, fangs, and rasplike hair. Despite this fearsome array of inborn weaponry it was reposing quietly on a bed of grass, half-asleep. Even at rest, though, this carnivore generated a sense of menace greater than any dozen terran tigers on the hunt.

"Though one of the fiercest and most unmanageable monsters living in your region of space, this creature too lives in peace and contentment in the private paradise which I create for it out of its own dreams."

"Good Minerva," McCoy suddenly blurted, staring at the cage and taking a step backwards, "it's a Capalent power-cat. No one's ever been able to keep one alive in captivity."

"I'm not familiar with the species, Bones," Kirk said, eyeing the cage respectfully. "Why haven't they?"

"They despise captivity, have to be killed before they can do any major damage," McCoy explained. "Try to confine them and they fly into a blind rage. That rage is coupled to generating cells that make a big electric eel's kick look like a communicator battery next to a warp-drive. One can put out enough juice to turn alloy-netting into a tin puddle, or kill a couple of dozen overenthusiastic hunters."

He looked up at Kukulkan. "I've never heard of one living in captivity for more than a couple of days. How did you manage to capture it in the first place?"

"This one was an infant, when encountered," the serpent told them, "and therefore more easily manipulated. As you were when first I visited Earth. You were destructive children who needed to be led."

"But if children are made totally dependent on their teachers," Kirk put in quickly, "they'll never be anything but children."

Alien wings ripped at the air. "Enough! This is use-less. Despite what I've told you, despite what you've seen, you persist in clinging to your disobedient ways." He swooped down to hover threateningly close.

"My dream is ending," he howled, "and all of you are to blame! No time," he continued with an ominous air of finality, "is ever given to those who must decide."

"Scatter!" Kirk yelled, reading Kukulkan's intentions in his tone. As the serpent dove at them the four officers did just that. The demigod hesitated, displaying something considerably short of omnipotence, trying to decide which of several ways to pursue first.

The question of the alien's omnipotence was one which had been burning in another mind for some time now. When the solution finally presented itself to Spock it gave support to the theory that what is most obvious is most often overlooked.

"Of course," he finally murmured softly. The elastic-ity of the force-field should not be able to respond to assault from more than a single source. If it could ab-sorb and redistribute phaser beams, it shouldn't be possible for it to simultaneously cope with opposing pressure from another source.

As always, he triple-checked his supposition with ac-tual math. The equations and conclusions which ap-peared on the library-computer screen confirmed his hopes.

He was speaking as he crossed to the empty com-mand chair. "All hands to battle stations . . . red alert is no longer on stand-by." Uhura complied and the fully activated triple shift readied for immediate action—all four hundred twenty-six of them.

"Full impulse power, Helmsman," he ordered in crisp tones as he settled himself in the chair. "Tractor beam on full power, warp-engines on stand-by."

A steady hum built on the Bridge as the closer im-pulse engine warmed.

"Tractor beam activated, sir," came the report from the engineering station.

"Very well. Set for maximum pull in precise opposition to our present heading."

"Aye, aye," came a ready but slightly confused voice.

"Mr. Arex, you are directed to compensate for catapult effect. When we break free of the confining force-field we will be thrown approximately five point seven light-years in a fraction of a second."

"Understood," the experienced navigator replied. Moments later he reported, "Catapult compensation factors laid in, sir. Gravity recoil compensation also checked."

"But how are we going to break free of the field?" Uhura wanted to know.

"This energy bubble, by its very nature, appears responsive to only one action per contained object, Lieutenant. If the same object—in this case, the *Enterprise*—both pushes and pulls on it simultaneously, at the same spot, the field should become sufficiently strained for a sudden burst of warp power to break clear of it.

"Mr. Sulu, Mr. Arex, you have our present spatial position?"

"Yes, sir," the double reply came. Spock wanted no chance of them being thrown nearly six light-years off with no way of relocating the alien's ship.

"Field contact with tractor beam in four seconds, sir," Arex announced. His voice was perhaps a twinge higher than usual.

Even as he finished, the *Enterprise,* in the person of its powerful tractor beam, once again encountered the restrictive surface of the force globe. Both tractor and impulse engine fought the same section of surface . . . pushing and pulling toward the identical end.

Spock didn't intend that they should bear the terrific strain very long. For one thing the tractor mechanism would blow up if it was required to pull against the opposing force of the impulse engine for more than a couple of minutes.

"Full warp power on my order," Spock said, shaping the syllables slowly. "Now."

Within the force globe the tubularnacelles housing

the great engines glowed brightly at the ends. The *Enterprise* hung in that nexus of antagonistic energies for a split second before a blinding white flash obliterated it from view.

Only a translucent blue globe remained.

In an empty, uncontested corner of space the flash was repeated for an audience of indifferent stars. The *Enterprise* appeared in its center. Kukulkan's ship was off the scanners.

No one raised a shout, there were no hysterical cheers. Those could wait until later, when the missing four crew members had been rescued.

"All decks report no damage, no injuries, sir," Uhura announced.

"Mr. Sulu, come about. Mr. Arex, put us on course to return." Spock betrayed no hint of satisfaction. His tone was no different than it had been when they had seemed hopelessly trapped.

By interstellar standards the distance they had to travel was not great. "Reduce speed to maximum close-range attack velocity, Mr. Sulu. Begin spiral attack pattern four. Arm all phasers and the photon torpedo banks."

"Sir," Sulu murmured, "if the Captain, Dr. McCoy and the others are still alive, wouldn't it be wise to . . .?"

"One of the hallmarks of wisdom is the assignment of priorities, Mr. Sulu. The *Enterprise* comes first. You will arm as directed."

"Yes, sir," came the flat response.

Thus prepared to deal a hurricane of destruction at the first attempt to encase them in another force-field, the *Enterprise* wound its way back toward the inimical ghost. . . .

Kirk was nearly exhausted. Just behind him, McCoy appeared to be in even worse shape. He glanced back and made a gesture. McCoy nodded in return. As they rounded the next suitable corner, both men dove behind one of the lowest of the suspended cages.

A writhing shape flashed by moments later, tongue flicking rapidly in all directions and red eyes glaring vengefully. Kirk marveled at the abilities of a race which could create technological wonders like this ship without the evolutionary benefit of manipulative members.

Surely those wings had always been wings, nor were there signs of rudimentary legs. The tail appeared reasonably prehensile, but that hardly seemed sufficient. Yet Kukulkan's people had managed, even triumphed, in matters of fine construction.

Even as he thought they had thrown off pursuit, bat-wings backed air and the twisting figure paused in mid-flight.

Kirk held his breath. He needn't have. It wasn't sudden detection of their presence that had brought Kukulkan to such an abrupt stop. Confusion of a different kind was apparent in his manner, and in the words he muttered unconsciously.

"Something is wrong."

Both officers hazarded a peek around the cage as the serpent made an elaborate gesture with both wings. A square of shimmering blackness materialized before him.

Looking into that was like peering into a cube of space. Miniature stars gleamed within it. Some were occluded by a miniature *Enterprise*.

And no force bubble encased it, Kirk noted excitedly.

The three-dimensional image of the ship grew larger and larger, until it seemed it would burst the confines of the cube.

"Escaped," Kukulkan was growling. "How? I will smash it this time . . ."

"Broken free, Jim!" McCoy exclaimed. "Spock . . ."

Kirk cut him off. "We've got to distract this thing and give him some time to get within range before another force bubble is projected—or worse." He started to draw back into the shadows, bumped something round and unyielding with his shoulder.

As the thought cleared he forgave himself the bruise. The exchange could be more than fair. "Bones, what would happen if we were to pull the cables on some of these cages? Disrupt the peaceful environments?"

McCoy shrugged. "Probably most of the animals

would just lie still. Those that weren't cowed would be too confused by the sudden change to know what to do. A few might react blindly . . ." A look of comprehension dawned on his face. "A few . . . the Capalent power-cat!"

"Come on, Bones . . ."

Keeping to the shadows, of which there were precious few because of the even illumination, they traced an indirect path back to the cage holding the big carnivore.

That belligerent creature was awake now and calmly preening itself. As they neared the cage, Kirk found himself wondering if this was really such a brilliant idea. Yet what else could they try? It would take a major disturbance to draw Kukulkan's considerable mind away from the approach of the *Enterprise*.

Kirk carried out a last experiment by charging straight at the cage and slamming his hands hard against the transparent-seeming side. Within, the power-cat's gaze moved directly to him—and past.

They'd have a chance, then. Moving around the cage they started tugging and pulling at the twin cables. Despite their most strenuous efforts, the connections held fast.

Well behind their present location, Kukulkan hovered in humid air and studied the newly created image of the *Enterprise*. He appeared to hear something, his head suddenly lifting and turning in several directions before settling on one.

"No, stop!" he commanded angrily, with perhaps a touch of something other than anger in that shout. Wings flapping furiously, he streaked off down one winding path. Behind him, now devoid of control, the black cube of shrunken universe broke up into tiny puffs of dark smoke.

Kirk heard that shout. Holding tight to the cable just past where it joined the black box beneath the cage floor, he tensed himself for a last, supreme effort.

He put his left foot up against the cage on one of the cable, and shoved. Maintaining pressure brought his right leg off the ground and planted the other side of the link. Suspended off the grou strained shoulders and legs at the same time. McCoy struggled to imitate his actions.

Kirk's cable gave with a snap and tiny shower of sparks. He fell to the ground. Seconds later, McCoy joined him. The doctor was no athlete, but he knew exactly how to utilize the combination of bands and ropes that made up the muscular system.

Both men employed that system to roll beneath the only immediate cover—the dark bottom of the cage itself.

Above their heads, reaction was instantaneous. The power-cat jerked back from what must have been a shocking and radical alteration of the landscape.

Spinning, it saw more of the same. It shrank down into the earthen floor of the now fully transparent cage. But when no further metamorphosis followed, it rose rapidly to all fours. It could see other creatures moving about around it. Air still pulsed through its lungs, its heart still beat. It was alive.

There is practically nothing a Capalent power-cat fears. Whether panic or rage or both motivated it then, neither Kirk nor McCoy could tell.

It rose up on its hind legs, fur bristling, fangs bared. They couldn't hear the snarl it made, because it was drowned by a greater explosion. The interior of the cage was filled with a violent discharge of electricity that shattered the walls and ceiling of the enclosure into a thousand fragments.

They could hear the snarling now, uncomfortably close above them—a deep-throated, angry rasp that cut the air like a scythe. The power-cat leaped clear and began prowling among the surrounding cages, throwing off immense bursts of energy like a four-_____ed hairy thunderhead.

_____ndom bolts struck the floor and ceiling of the _____r. Where they made contact, deep smoking _____ the material appeared. Other bursts shattered _____s, sending the respective inhabitants into _____sis or leaping for the nearest shelter.

_____he rampaging killer's discharges seemed _____tensity. It reached the point where each _____ed the color of the room to change. Kirk could feel the hair on his arms and the back of his neck stand on end in the presence of so much unchanneled power.

Kukulkan was close by, but he was no longer concerned with Kirk and McCoy, nor with Scott and Walking Bear who had hurried to the region of disturbance to offer aid if either captain or physician were in danger.

Wings fluttered in agitation as the serpent hissed, "Irrational savages! See what you have done!"

"Prepare to fire, Mr. Sulu," Spock ordered calmly as the range to the ghost ship closed. "Aim for the propulsion units."

"Aye, sir."

They swept close ... and no force-field appeared to meet them. No duplicate of the pure white energy beam leaped to strike at their deflector shields.

"Fire, Mr. Sulu. Phasers first."

Twin beams of blue energy crossed the distance between ships. This time there was nothing to stop them. They raked the alien's drive.

"Again, Mr. Sulu." Once more the rear section of Kukulkan's vessel was hit.

Within the life-room a brief turquoise glow touched everything. Then all was plunged into darkness in which the only light came from luminescent specimens and the intermittent blaze of the power-cat.

The carnivore's snarls reached them above an increasing mélange of squeaks, chirps, moans and whistles. Kirk decided to take a chance, crawled clear of the protective cage. To the power-cat, his yell should be no more distracting than the calls of any other freed creatures.

"Kukulkan! You can't control one of your *own* creatures!" The emphasis on the *own* was intentional, but the irony was wasted on that monumental reptilian ego.

Light returned to the chamber and Kirk ducked back out of sight. But this wasn't the bright, powerful illumination of before. It was dim and flickered dimmer

at random moments. It was strong enough for them to
see by with reasonable ease, though.

Kukulkan had made no attempt to locate the source
of that taunt. Instead, he was shrinking back against
one smoking cage as the odor of crisped air drifted
back to them. Both cat and prey were edging toward
their hiding place.

"I cannot, any longer. Your ship has crippled my
central power source."

Kirk was about to say something about the power of
a god, but McCoy had grabbed his arm. "If that's true,
Jim, then that cat's a real threat to all of us."

A snarl sounded close by, and a moment later
Kukulkan appeared. The power-cat had its head down
and was stalking the serpent-god with single-minded
hatred. It was backing Kukulkan in against a shattered
cage that reached nearly to the ceiling. Its tail lashed
back and forth and blue sparks danced on its fur.
Ozone stank in their nostrils.

"We've got to do something, Jim, it'll be after us
next."

"Your medikit, Bones—maximum tranquilizer set-
ting for alien mammaloids."

McCoy was fumbling at his kit instantly, muttering.
"We're not certain it's a mammal, Jim. Power-cat
study's not a favorite subject among researchers on Capalent. I don't even know if the hypo will penetrate."

"It better," Kirk warned nervously.

McCoy drained nearly all of one vial to fill the hypo,
then slapped it into Kirk's ready palm like a relay run-
ner's baton. Kirk was already dashing from their hiding
place before the doctor could think to object.

Kukulkan was lashing his tail like a whip and
beating with its wings. The power-cat was not
impressed. If the serpent tried to dodge, the cat would
cut him off to either side ... and there wasn't enough
room to fly over the towering cage. Escape was impossible.

Powerful leg muscles tightened and the carnivore's
tail twitched faster. It was readying itself to spring,
eyes fixed on the brightly-colored creature which hov-

ered before it. One might think the position of deity
and mortal had been reversed.

So intent was it upon Kukulkan that the power-cat
never saw Kirk. The captain brandished the hypo like
a knife and slammed it into the carnivore's rear right
hip.

It whirled immediately, as much startled as angered.
The burst of electricity it threw off was reflexive rather
than directed. That saved Kirk's life. The discharge
was still powerful enough to send him flying into a
nearby tangle of uncaged shrubs.

Apparently unhurt, the cat readied itself to hurl a
better-aimed charge at this tiny new opponent. Instead,
it shook its head and got down off its hind legs, eyes
blinking slowly.

Behind it, Kukulkan's agitation diminished. The god
cocked his head quizzically as he evaluated the change
in the now dazed killer. Its gaze rose to study the place
where Kirk lay.

McCoy was at the captain's side in a moment, but
Kirk was evidently all right. He was sitting up, shaking
his head and rubbing at his right shoulder. The doctor's voice was still concerned.

"Did you inject the beast or yourself? You look a
little rocky, Jim."

"I'm okay, Bones. That last bolt just singed me.
Funny stuff, lightning. It can turn a hundred-meter-tall
tree into lawn stakes without harming someone standing nearby." He gestured with his head to where a long
black streak had scorched the deck just to one side of
where he'd been, seconds before.

Okay or not, he didn't object when McCoy offered
him a hand up. The narrowness of his escape was mag-
nified when a few steps brought them to the hypo. It
had been thrown clear. It was recognizable as the hypo
only because it couldn't be anything else. Metal and
glass were fused into a vaguely cylindrical blob of still
hot slag.

Kukulkan, meanwhile, had recovered enough to hover above the power-cat. Kirk considered running for
their hiding place, then shrugged. They'd already been

seen and anyway, with the power-cat immobilized, the serpent could locate them at its leisure.

McCoy joined him as he walked toward the carnivore. The huge creature was not unconscious. It possessed physical reserves which could almost handle even the massive dose it had been injected with. It sat swaying slightly and licking its forepaws.

"What a system!" McCoy murmured in admiration. "That hypo had enough mynoquintistrycnite in it to knock out a herd of hippos."

"It's just like a big kitten," a voice sounded behind them. Walking Bear, and Scott with him. The first animal they had seen, the lumbering platypus-like thing, was waddling behind Scott. Every once in a while it would sidle up next to him and rub up and down his leg like a big slick dog, uttering a peculiar gulping sound.

Scott would hesitate, then reach down to scratch behind its ears. "What's this, again? Aren't you the friendly little darlin'."

"Hello Walking Bear, Scotty," Kirk hailed.

"I see things have calmed down a bit, Captain," Scott observed with satisfaction, staring past him. "Maybe now all concerned parties can discuss things a bit more sensibly."

"Yes," Kirk agreed, turning to face Kukulkan. "I think we've earned the right to be heard."

"You continue to take advantage of me," the serpent replied grudgingly. "Yet my beamed request for time will not delay your Mr. Spock much longer. He would destroy my ship. Therefore I must consent. Speak what you will."

Kirk nodded back to where Scott was still scratching the alien platypus. The eyes of the creature were closed in apparent pleasure.

"You think of us as being weak, small creatures like that one, as unintelligent animals. Are we truly that inferior to you?" Kukulkan paused, seeming for the first time to consider his reply before speaking.

"Potentially, mentally . . . no. But compared to the violence of your kind, the power-cat in its natural state is docility personified. How can I let that live to poison an unsuspecting universe?"

McCoy's hands were locked behind his back. He was rocking slowly on his heels and staring expectantly at Kirk. Obviously the good doctor was burning to say something. Kirk saw no reason to stand in his way.

"We'd be fools if we didn't learn from our own history," McCoy began. "Those minds you admit aren't so inferior to yours ... we've been using them since you last visited us. Don't let your probe's tales of warships and arms convince you we're about to embark on a Galaxywide war of extermination. We've been working to bring about a multiracial civilization in which everyone can live in peace with his neighbors. We've already accomplished this within our own Federation." He grinned. "A few persistent throwbacks like the Klingons and Romulans will come around, in time."

"You see why we can't be what you originally intended for us," Kirk continued. "If we fail or succeed, it has to be—*must* be—by our own hands. By our own doing.

"You could probably find your worshipful servant races somewhere, Kukulkan, but they'd have to be blind and dumb. Once you have a being with a mind of its own, you can no longer lead it around by the nose. You cannot have intelligent slaves, Kukulkan. The thing is as impossible as a leisurely cruise past a black hole."

Kirk didn't think it was possible for that cobra countenance to look downcast, but Kukulkan managed it.

"I thought of you as my children. I hoped I could teach you, lead you, aid you. There is much I can ..."

"You already have," Kirk said, with more compassion than he believed he could muster for this overbearing creature. "Long ago, when it was needed most —when our ancestors were still children. But we're all grown up now, Kukulkan."

He hesitated, then added as gently as possible, "We don't need you anymore."

This time the serpent spoke with true somberness. "It seems I have already done what I can, and things cannot be as I wished them. Therefore ... I will let

you go your own way, as you wish." The power-cat
had ceased licking itself and now lay down peacefully
between them.

"We would still have you as a friend and equal,
Kukulkan," Kirk offered.

"No ... no." The wings beat slowly. "That cannot
be, now, for me. As you cannot be servants and children, so can I be no less than the master. It is sad, but
it is truth.

"Go now ... "

Kirk studied the viewscreen. Kukulkan's ship still
hovered there, but its awesome energy cloak was gone.
The need for deception had passed.

McCoy stood nearby while Spock was watching the
screen from his position at the library-computer station.

"An interesting experience," the first officer observed.

"Interesting," McCoy mumbled, in a tone that indicated he would have used other adjectives to describe
what they had just been through.

"Our visitor turned out to be the actual Mayan god,"
Spock concluded.

"And the Toltecs' Quetzalcoatl," Walking Bear reminded, "and the original Chinese dragon, and all the
rest."

"But not quite a god," Kirk corrected them. "Just an
old, lonely being who wanted to help others—an ego-
maniacal hermit who'd chose isolation before confess-
ing to his mortality."

McCoy grinned and crossed his arms, rather like a
gunfighter preparing for a standoff—only the doctor
was readying a verbal salvo.

"Spock," he began innocently, "I don't suppose Vulcans have legends like those?"

The first officer regarded him evenly, raised one eyebrow. "Not legends, Doctor. Vulcan *was* visited by
alien beings in its past. They, however, left us much
wiser."

McCoy was preparing a reply when Arex, who had
insisted on remaining on duty until the incident was fi-

nally resolved, broke in with a report.

"The other vessel is getting under way, sir, heading directly outward along the transmission heading."

"Away from Earth, away from the Federation," Kirk confirmed, watching as Kukulkan's ship began to shrink on the screen. "It's sad. Think what we could do with the knowledge on that ship, held in that mind." He shook his head.

"Unfortunately, the price was just too high."

"I think I know how he felt, Jim," McCoy commented, turning suddenly serious. Spock also turned to look at him. "There's a line from Shakespeare . . ."

"I remember it, too, Bones." Kirk's voice recited, " 'How sharper than a serpent's tooth it is to have a thankless child'."

"Indeed, Captain," Spock agreed, filling that terse comment with more meaning than most people could put in several paragraphs.

Kirk sighed, looked back at the screen. It was empty again, empty save for that endless panoply of marching suns. They glowed mockingly back at him, each holding secrets they stubbornly guarded with distance and time.

"Lay in a course for Starbase 21, Mr. Arex. All ahead warp-three . . ."